# Tails Always Wins

By

I0527421

## C. A. King

**Cover Design:**

**Jennifer Munswami**
**–**
**J.M. Rising Horse Creations**

**Editor:**

**Karen Hrdlicka**

*If you believe this book is dedicated to you,*

*perhaps it is!*

Cover Design: Jennifer Munswami - J.M. Rising Horse Creations

First Printing: May 2019,

Reprint: September 2019

ISBN: 978-1-988301-78-5

Kings Toe Publishing

kingstoepublishing@gmail.com

Brantford, Ontario. Canada

# *Chapter One*

Snow was a liar and possibly the biggest one in existence. It fell softly from the heavens in the form of angel wings: delicate and beautiful. Each flake touched down with the weight of a feather, forming a blanket wherever it landed. It had all the makings of a cozy bed: soft, warm, and inviting. The truth was, though, a million feathers wasn't light and those covers weren't warm. Even its pearly clean appearance was deceiving. White suggested purity. In reality, the frosty flakes were merely a mask—a disguise for the dirt and grime hiding beneath and within. The ground it fell on was Mother Nature's version of a masquerade ball.

The surface of the freshly fallen powder already had a crunch to it, even beneath the tiniest of feet. Brodie stumbled forward, his shoe remaining in the last footprint he left. The horizon was a blank canvas waiting for colour to be added. A torrential downpour of confetti whipped at exposed skin, making sure all who ventured in its path knew this was no dream.

The mangled car, left only a few steps back, was almost gone—hidden by nature's clean-up crew. He was the only thing not affected. Jack Frost was no match for a healthy shifter's metabolism. Even at the tender age of eight, his temperature ran high, thawing anything frosty thrown his way. That took care of Brodie's immediate physical problems. His injuries were only surface deep, other than shock and grief.

Brodie fell to his knees, tears burning a hole in the shimmering surface of the ground beneath him. The wind growled, slapping him across the face for his weakness, before picking up death's scent. With bigger fish to fry, a weeping child wasn't worth the effort. The next gusts declared the swirling storm a murderer. Brodie threw back his head and let out a hair-curdling howl, arguing with the reaper himself, but to no avail. His parents had been killed and it probably was all his fault.

The tempest's direction changed. Laughter echoed, carried on every gust. The trees swayed, branches cracking their amusement. The tempo of the symphony mocking his pain grew louder with death standing tall as its conductor.

Brodie curled up into a ball, waiting for his turn to be carried away to the afterlife, but no one came for him. There was to be no relief from his agony. The insides of his eyelids played a looping vision of flames burning all that he knew. His home, his toys, his safety net; all turned to ash. When he opened them again, there was no blur to his sight. Cold reality loomed overhead, declaring itself the victor in a game he never chose to play; one he never had a chance to win.

Brodie's heart ached, longing for the embrace only a mother or father could give. His cries remained unanswered. Shivers ran down his spine, branching to each and every extremity in his small body. Fear found a home in his soul and had taken up residence faster than the blink of an eye, inviting guilt as its first visitor.

Brodie gulped back the lump forming in his throat. If this were his fault, he'd make sure it never happened again. A silent vow became a life-long promise. It was ironic, really. Performing a full shift not only gave him full control over his abilities, but was also the sole reason why it could never happen again. No one else would end up in an untimely grave because of what he was.

Loud footsteps trudged through the drifts, heading his way. The powers that be had delivered their verdict, allowing him another chance at life. A glimmer of hope ignited in Brodie's soul, that one, if not both, of his parents were given the same reprieve. Perhaps they were still among the living.

That was life's cruel joke, lending hope—then snatching it away again—snickering at the anguish it caused. For Brodie, such optimism extinguished the moment a pair of chilled arms lifted him. Even through the raging storm, he recognized the scent of a man his parents had called a friend.

There was little solace in knowing he was safe. He'd survived, but everything he knew was gone. He buried his face in the man's jacket, melting the layer of snow that had accumulated on it.

"It's okay," the man said. "There was a bad accident, but I've got you. I'm going to take you home tonight and tomorrow we can figure everything out."

Brodie listened to his voice, but didn't respond. The meaning lying in between the man's words confirmed his worst fears. Even the young understood the finality that came with death's icy grip. There had been other relatives that he'd seen pass on. Once life ceased, it couldn't be brought back. That was the one true law of the universe. No one could sort that out. Death was forever. He would never see his parents again.

He glanced over the man's shoulders at the pile of white that had been his family car. Tears flowed freely down his cheeks for those being left behind. He closed his eyes tight, trying to save a picture of their faces. He needed to hang onto their memory. It was all he had left. Time became the new villain. As days, weeks, months, and years passed, he'd slowly begin to forget. Their smiles and voices would be lost among those of countless other souls. That fate, no one deserved, especially not them.

He reached out, grabbing a hold of a fistful of snowflakes to save the moment. By the time he opened his hand; they too were gone.

# *Chapter Two*

*Twenty years later...*

Brodie opened the summons for the hundredth time. The contents hadn't changed; that included his name in its entirety printed front and centre on the paper. It was all legal: signed, sealed, and delivered by a well-known local county judge. He had been not-so-cordially invited to attend a meeting at the Samson Recreational Facility. The purpose of said meeting, however, had been omitted. Mysteries always spelt trouble.

Not knowing what was happening meant surrendering control to someone else. That wasn't easy for anyone harbouring an alpha male personality. He'd managed to suppress his dominant side before, but he wasn't sure that would always be the case. The pungent scent of strife in the air already had him on edge. Something terrible was coming, and he needed to stay razor-sharp if he was going to have any chance of avoiding being caught smack dab in the middle of it.

Normally, Brodie would have hailed a taxi and arrived in style. That night wasn't meant for fancy rides, though. His tolerance levels were trending toward the lower portion of the placidity charts. A long walk in the frigid February temperatures was the only thing that was going to cool him off.

To him, the pace he set was slow and methodical. To any normal person, he was speed walking. That was only one of the differences between shifters and the rest of society. His strut came to a crawl, nearing his destination.

Anxiety attempted a forceful takeover, upping the ante in its bid for control. Tiny beads of sweat formed on Brodie's brow. He swatted them away with one hand as he passed by the entrance of the building several times before garnering enough nerve to head to the front door. Once the path was chosen, he moved swiftly, long legs taking two of the concrete steps at a time.

A vending machine was another opportunity to stall. It had been strategically placed outside, drawing in the spare change of anyone entering as well as those heading out. He shoved his hand in his pocket, pulling out the contents. One finger moved around the treasures it retrieved.

"Damn," he muttered. There wasn't enough to buy even a single stick of gum, let alone a whole pack. His dry mouth was on the verge of expressing its feelings, using an array of profane words. A large coin clanged, dropping into the mix in his palm. Brodie's gaze slowly shifted upward.

"You look like you could use it," the woman said. "It's Tails, by the way." The silver in her eyes shimmered, glistening in the last of the day's light. Their icy beauty sent shivers down his spine. Everything about her spelled trouble; including the sweet floral scent that remained behind to tease his senses. She was one mystery he wouldn't mind unravelling, even if it did come with a side order of trouble.

Brodie glanced down. "It isn't," he argued. "It's actually heads." He chuckled, taking another glimpse of the shiny round piece. "Wait! How'd you do that?" The coin had flipped—tails side up. He scratched his head, swearing it had been heads before.

His eyes shifted, catching only a glimpse of the woman's backside strutting away. Long hair swished in time with her hips, leaving him mesmerized by an array of soft pastel colours. He opened his mouth to call out, but before another syllable formed, the building's double doors were swinging shut.

A frown etched its way onto his face. He might not have put on his Sunday best, but he certainly wasn't a charity case. His free hand rubbed the stubble on his chin. He probably should have taken the time to shave before attending the meeting. Of course, he hadn't expected to meet anyone worth making an effort for. This woman, whoever she was, had made quite the first impression, and from what he had seen, was definitely deserving of his further attention.

He glanced down at the money she'd tossed him. The gesture was nothing more than a plastic bone to a starving dog. Still, it was more than anyone had offered him freely in a long time. He cupped his hand, breathing into it. The sniff test was all he needed to make a decision. He needed the gum more than water, especially if he planned on doing any talking at all. Bad breath was offensive in any circle. Chewing took care of offensive odours and his dry mouth and throat to boot.

Package in hand, Brodie fiddled with the wrapping. The little red line taunted him. Not only was red a trigger colour for all shifters, especially those attempting to deal with inner struggles over suppressing their true natures, but the stupid piece of plastic had no end. It wasn't supposed to take a rocket scientist to open a piece of candy. It was literally child's play. The strip was designed to easily lift, creating an opening in the packaging around the top of the gum. This one didn't do that. His fingers fumbled, searching for the end to tug at, to no avail. He gave in, his teeth gnawing at the plastic until it tore. Bits of wrapper spat onto the ground.

The shiny silver foil of the first stick reflected the light of the moon. Saliva flowed into his mouth, anticipating the flavour that was about to come. His tongue darted out to share the moisture with both of his lips. The froth and drool of a ravenous scavenger on the prowl for a meal ran down his chin, lending him the appearance of a rabid animal. Looks were deceiving, though. All he wanted was the fresh tingle only peppermint could provide. He wiped his face with a sleeve, hoping no one had been watching.

"Ah," he said, relishing the taste. The rest of the packet disappeared into his front pocket for easy access later, if needed.

His hand froze on the door handle. A poorly designed sign had been stuck in full view: *AAA meeting in room 101.*

Brodie glanced at the paper summons, remembering the number it cited. They were the same. It had to be a mistake. He wasn't by any means an alcoholic. In fact, he prided himself on being strong enough to not need sedation in order to handle everyday life. His head shook as the door swung open. At the very least, he needed to clear up whatever blunders some city official had made.

Brodie found himself staring at the second door. It was proving no easier to enter than the first one had been. He'd gotten by it riding on the back of sheer pride. This one required a little more nerve and a little less emotion.

A water fountain was the perfect way to elude the task at hand. He bent over at the waist, turning the handle slightly. Taps gone crazy were an ongoing theme in his life. They had it out for him, even if there was always a technical explanation for any of malfunctions that happened. He knew all about the soakings a single loose screw was able to cause. It was the number of times plumbing problems happened in his presence that made him skeptical another force wasn't behind the issues. Simply having a magnetic personality shouldn't have an affect on metal.

The water trickled upward, forming an arch. Chapped lips absorbed the first touches of moisture before parting to allow the full flow to pass. The volume of his slurps increased with every passerby. Technically, he was at the meeting. He side-eyed his watch, his mouth still taking in liquid. It was still a few minutes early.

Being late was the worst thing he could do. There was no need to point himself out to anyone who hadn't noticed him in the first place. The back of the room was the place for him—out of sight—out of mind.

A second stick of gum folded between his teeth. Even he could only handle so much water before becoming bogged down by its weight. His stomach swished as he waddled his way to the door and glanced inside.

An elderly man had claimed the spot at the front of the room. Chairs had been neatly arranged opposite to his. The only other person present was the woman from outside. He shoved both his hands in his pockets; shoulders slumped. This was the perfect chance to sort out the details of the summons and be out of there before anyone else arrived. All he needed was the nerve. A push on his back served the same purpose. He stumbled forward, stopping short of the evening's organizer.

"Can I help you?" the man asked, his voice monotone.

Brodie cleared his throat with a brisk cough into his hand. "Yes," he answered. "I received this." The letter waved high above his head. It was a white flag blowing in the wind and was taken as his surrender.

"Have a seat," the man ordered.

Brodie flinched. He glanced over his shoulder at the two seats already occupied. The muscular man who pushed past him had joined the circus they had all been sold to. "I was wondering what, exactly, this meeting was about. I think there may have been a mistake. I'm not a substance abuser."

The audience laughed in the background.

"No one said you were." The man tossed his glasses on a desk and glanced up. The white of his hair matched that growing out of both of his nostrils. They flared at the disruption, providing an even better view inside each. "I take it you are referring to the paper stuck to the door. That isn't ours. Good help is hard to find these days. At least, when looking outside the human race." He returned his glasses to his face and his attention to his paperwork. "Cheap labour isn't always better."

"Sorry," Brodie pressed on. "What is this meeting for? The summons doesn't actually say."

The man's mouth twitched, a sigh pushing its way passed his lips. "This is an anger management class. I trust you won't be giving me any problems this evening. Leave your summons on the desk and take a seat." His voice rose with every word. "I'll explain more when the rest of your pack arrives."

"My pack?" Brodie echoed, his face wrinkling with confusion. "I don't have a pack." The hairs on his arms stood at attention, warning of confrontation looming overhead.

The man's glasses landed with a thump on the desk. They were taking the brunt of his anger. "I've had enough out of you. Take a seat or I will call the authorities. I deal with your sort all the time. I am not about to let you lose control and injure anyone. Are we clear?"

Brodie stood still for a moment processing the information. None of it made sense. He was being as reasonable as possible under the circumstances. The man before him was the one in need of a few anger management sessions.

"Are we clear?" the man bellowed, standing up. His hands came down heavy on the desk, knocking his glasses flying.

"No," Brodie muttered.

"Pardon?!" the man yelled. "You dare defy me?"

Brodie's voice rose for the first time since being a child. "I haven't done anything to warrant being in this class. I am trying to explain there has been a misunderstanding. The least you could do is acknowledge the possibility and look into it further." His hand formed a fist worthy of battle, knuckles turning white.

The man threw his head back, howling a laugh, which sounded anything but human. "You insolent pest," he scoffed, slapping his inferior across the face.

Brodie's face shifted sideways from the jolt. His fist rose, primed to take action. The follow though stuttered, leaving his hand hanging. His arm fell back to his side. Violence was never the solution to any argument.

"Striking an anger management instructor is a serious offence," the man said, a sly grin plastered over his face. He lifted his finger, accentuating its downward motion as it pressed on a large red button, summoning help.

"I didn't hit you," Brodie argued. "I stopped short."

"You lost your temper," the man replied, chuckling. "Your type always does. There's no helping any of you deal with your rage. This farce of a class is merely a formality. You'll all be locked away soon enough."

It took less than a minute for two officers to appear, weapons at the ready. "Freeze!" they demanded in unison.

That was another command that didn't make sense. Brodie hadn't moved a muscle since threatening to strike. He held his hands out in the least threatening manner he knew, but it made no difference. The next thing he felt was a jolt of electricity and a thump on the back of his head. As he fell, his eyes connected with the woman he never had the opportunity to meet. A rainbow of colours glossed over his vision; the same soft pastels that highlighted her hair. He tried to blink off fainting, yearning for a couple more glimpses.

# Chapter Three

Staying calm in a den of predators wasn't the easiest task. Losing his temper was what landed Brodie in this situation in the first place. It was the first and only time he'd raised a hand to anyone. Even then, he managed to stop before dealing a blow. Apparently, scaring the piss out of someone was enough to land a guy in jail.

He inhaled deeply, soothing his inner beast. Once arrested, it became obvious the powers that were in charge had no plans on letting him loose again. Everything around him was meant to aggravate, from the metal cuffs restraining his hands and legs, to the bright orange colour of the jumper he was forced to wear—all teasers for his other nature. It was working, too. The primal urges of an animal were winning over humanity.

Another direct hit to his psyche and he was bound to lose control.

"Just a few more hours," Brodie mumbled to himself. If he could make it through the worst would be behind him. This whole mess was, after all, nothing more than a misunderstanding. He hadn't done anything wrong. Any judge was sure to see that and release him with a slap on the wrist. He wasn't a criminal.

Two guards in full riot gear appeared at the door to his cell. The hairs on the back of Brodie's neck stood up, a warning that masked faces held no emotion. A cross between a baton and a Taser banged between two of the bars that separated man and accused. The sound radiated through the facility, eliciting a range of howls in response. Neither guard uttered a word. Animals were expected to obey unspoken commands. If they didn't know how to, there was extensive training available one cell block over. Nightly cries of inmates in anguish were a strong behavioural motivator for others.

Brodie let out a breath of air in a quick huff. The baton twirled and he followed the command. With arms outstretched, he shuffled his feet in a circular motion. It wasn't a runway model twirl by any means, but it was the best he could perform in shackles.

The black stick banged three times. It was time to step back and allow the guards to enter for a more thorough inspection. If he hadn't seen the whole process happen the day before to the prisoner beside him, he never would have understood what the nonverbal instructions meant. All methods of teaching carried out in the joint involved extreme violence. Brodie had chosen to live his entire life as a pacifist and had no plans to change that anytime soon.

The two masked men poked and prodded him in a fashion that wasn't fit for cattle being taken for slaughter. Each jab came with an undeserved bolt of electricity. There was no need to see their faces to know the smirk they wore. Ironically, cruelty was a human trait; beasts were more humane in comparison.

Disappointment lingered in the silence that followed. A push sent Brodie stumbling forward. If he fell on the grey concrete flooring, one part of him or another was bound to end up broken. Most likely his nose. Quick reflexes jumped to the rescue, averting the danger. It wasn't the last hard knock the two would dole out, though. There was a long walk between cell and courtroom and there was bound to be plenty of opportunity.

Brodie's head remained down, forming the most submissive position possible. Admitting the law was alpha male was the key to his defence. That he figured out himself, without a lawyer whispering it in his ear. Still, the sight of the old man waiting at the end of the tunnel was a needed breath of fresh air. A better barrister and solicitor he couldn't have hoped for.

Gerald Fitzsimons was not only a respected attorney, he was a close friend. After Brodie's parents perished in the accident, he took it upon himself to keep tabs on Brodie. His legal services hadn't been required until that moment.

"You don't look too worse for wear, considering," Gerald said, pointing to a chair. "Have a seat. I need to go over your case before the trial."

"Trial?" Brodie questioned, his brows arched high enough to form peaks. "Why would this be going to trial? No crime was committed. I didn't do anything."

Gerald glanced up from his paperwork, his expression solemn. "That's for the courts to decide. In particular—Judge Hawethorne. You need to keep quiet and let me do the talking." His arm extended; hand patting his client's arm.

"Hey," Brodie complained, turning his wrist to expose a clear patch of tape. "What's that for?"

"A little something to calm your nerves," Gerald whispered back. "It'll make a big difference this afternoon."

Brodie shook his head. "Do you know how much trouble I'll be in if they find out? Managing emotions with drugs is illegal for shifters. You should know that."

"So is hitting your anger management instructor," Gerald argued. "You managed to do that without any problem."

"What?!" Brodie exclaimed. "I didn't hit anyone. What happened to innocent before proven guilty? Aren't you supposed to give me the benefit of the doubt?"

"Wake up and smell the coffee," the attorney snorted. "I know they are serving that to you in prison. Caffeine gets your kind all riled up." He paused. "Things are changing and fast. The prosecutor has the testimony of the instructor and a broken pair of glasses from the assault as proof."

"He dropped the glasses himself," Brodie complained. "I am being set-up. Besides it is his word against mine."

"A human's word against yours," Gerald corrected. "Need I remind you? Being a shifter doesn't bode well for you in this matter."

"There were two other people in the room," Brodie said. "They both saw what happened. I admit I was upset and made a fist, but I never followed through. Did anyone even ask them?"

"Don't you get it?" Gerald replied, a sigh escaping with his words. "They are in the same boat as you. Neither of them are going to speak out against Dejardins. He's a respected scholar, well known for his research on animal agitation. Just raising your fist to him is a felony."

"I didn't do anything wrong," Brodie complained. "He was egging me on. Besides this is a first offence. You know I have never lost my cool before."

"But you did loose your cool," Gerald commented. "Once is too many times with the state of things at the moment."

"My neighbour has done worse—a thousand times over," Brodie scoffed. "You can't seriously believe they are going to lock me up and throw away the key for having one argument."

"The chap next door to you shifts into a house cat," Gerald replied. "That form is of no threat to anyone. He is literally a pussy. You, on the other hand, are a different story."

"What do you mean?" Brodie questioned, examining the chains that bound him. He tugged testing their strength.

"Don't you follow current events?" Gerald asked, one brow arched. He sighed at the head shake he received as a response. "You should."

"Why what happened?" Brodie questioned.

The attorney stood, one hand delved deep into the pocket of his suit pants. Jingling coins exposed his hidden fidgeting fingers. "Bill six-six-six passed at the beginning of the week."

"The Bill of the Beast," Brodie scoffed, adding a chuckle at the end. "That's a great name they chose."

"It's not funny," Gerald snapped. "That is exactly what it is. The old registries were deemed insufficient to provide safety for the human population. This bill allows for a registry for dangerous species. I'm afraid you fall on that list."

"Dangerous breeds?!" Brodie exclaimed. "You're kidding. It was bad enough when the human population wiped out various bloodlines of dogs. Now they want to do the same to people?"

"The bill also classifies those on it a sub-human," Gerald muttered. "It revokes many of your rights as a citizen."

"What rights?" Brodie questioned. The drug patch began to make sense. Had he not been administered a calming agent, his other side would have been hard to keep under wraps.

Gerald let out a huff. "Your voter registration has been revoked. You are no longer eligible for certain jobs. I have a printout of those for you. There are new laws to follow as well: a curfew to adhere to, a licence is required for breeding, and you can not display any form of aggravation in public."

"So if I don't do what I'm told like a good pet, I'll be put down?!" Brodie complained. "This is preposterous. I'm a living being."

"No one is challenging that," Gerald replied, his expression solemn. "What is in question is if your specific type is dangerous to society. There have been some cases as of late."

"Some cases?!" Brodie complained. "Humanity is known for their brutality. What gives them the right to condemn an entire species based on a few cases?"

"Don't shoot the messenger," the attorney suggested. "I don't like this anymore than you do. There are already protests taking place around the globe. That, however, doesn't help what happens in the meantime. You are about to stand trial and I, as your representative, can't allow you to make any outbursts in court. That would seal your fate. Let me do all the talking. You smile and agree with everything. Under no circumstances are you to engage in any disagreements. We may not like it, but for now, it is the only way to reduce the sentence."

"Sentence?!" Brodie, shrieked his voice cracking. "How can I have a sentence without having been before a judge yet?"

"Striking a human now carries a minimum year jail term," Gerald explained. His lips pursed together, sticking out slightly. "I think I can have it reduced to some form of community service, though. Leave it to me. No one is going to listen to you anyway."

"And if I don't?" Brodie muttered.

Gerald sighed. "There are already reports of the complete annihilation of the black bear shifter species. A bulletin is being posted bi-weekly updating extinctions. That's one list you don't want to find yourself on."

# Chapter Four

Zeus crossed his legs. He wasn't the type to be kept waiting, especially by a woman. He grasped the warmed snifter placed before him, swirling the caramel-coloured liquid inside. It was the perfect colour, no doubt darkened naturally from being properly aged in pure oak wooden barrels. At least someone managed to get his drink right.

With the edge of the glass almost touching his chin, he inhaled the dried fruit aromas that had concentrated at the top. The brim inched closer to his nostrils, each flaring its approval. He set the glass back down. Another scent had interfered with his ritual. This one was undeniably floral.

"You're late," he scoffed, folding his hands together.

A coin twirled high in the air, slapping hard on the back of her hand after being caught on its descent. There was no need to look to know which side was facing up. It was always the same. That was how she came about her name—after all—at least that was the story everyone knew. It was a tad bit easier than admitting she didn't have one or worse using Subject 247E.

"I had a few things to take care of," she replied, taking the chair across from him. "So tell me, what is so important you'd be seen with me in the middle of the day?"

Zeus chuckled. "Tails, you are a wildflower that any gardener would be proud to have growing among their award winning roses," he responded, sound waves doing his flirting for him.

"I'm way past falling for your charm," Tails snickered. "Let's drop the charade and get down to business. Why am I here?"

"You are here," Zeus replied, "because I need you here; our cause needs you here." He restarted his drinking ritual from the beginning. "Your enticing scent isn't as strong as it used to be. My spirits almost outshine you."

The rim of his cup pressed against his mouth. The first sip was nothing more than a tease, enough to wet his lips, but allowing only the smallest amount to actually pass through. He closed his eyes, savouring the burn on the tip of his tongue. The corners of his mouth curled up, an offering of appreciation for the finely crafted French brandy and an equally well-crafted woman. He eyed her up and down, taking in every curve. The teasing wink she offered in return burnt in a similar manner to the alcohol, although not in his mouth. She knew exactly how to get a man riled up and that was exactly why he kept her around.

"I'm not here to play," Tails stated.

"What fun is that?" Zeus teased. "We have my whole club to ourselves. I do miss our afternoon romps." He howled a laugh. "You've lost your sense of adventure." His glass pressed between his lips, allowing the liquid to flow through, this sip considerably larger than the last.

Tails glanced around the posh room that normally only catered to the rich and famous. The chandelier hanging overhead alone was worth more than every item she owned put together. Many an evening had been spent dancing the night away in the arms of the man she faced. Back then, money and a safe haven had been her only motive. It didn't hurt that Zeus was easy on the eyes, a silver fox in every manner. Things were different now; she was different and she wasn't for sale.

Zeus sighed, growing weary of her silence. "Very well," he grumbled, waving his hand through the air. "What went wrong at the meeting? I didn't receive a report."

"I didn't realize a simple case of shifter injustice warranted a report," Tails replied. "I don't even know who he was. It was his first night."

"Well I do!" Zeus exclaimed. "That fellow is one of the most important pieces on our chessboard. The fact he fell into our hands and then right through our fingers again is preposterous." He pulled on the silk ascot wrapped around his neck, feeling the weight of her stare.

"What is so important about this guy?" Tails questioned. "We don't usually go out on a limb for a single shifter. What aren't you telling me?" The smell of deceit filled the air; a scent she knew all to well.

"You know as well as I do, there are things we can't explain in this world," Zeus replied. "Look at you for instance. Why do men drop at your feet with a bat of your eyes?"

"What does he do?" Tails asked, rolling his eyes.

"I can't tell you that," Zeus answered. "All I can say is that he has an important role to play, and we need him to do it willingly. That's where you come in."

"Really?" Tails snickered. She stood; ready to walk away.

Zeus's hand came down hard on her arm, latching on in a death grip. "This is not negotiable." A single push sent her flying back into the seat.

"I don't like being manhandled," Tails complained.

Zeus chuckled. "I guess it is a good thing I'm not a man then." A sly grin formed over his lips. One hand shook a silver bell, alerting his staff he required a new drink.

"What is it you expect me to do?" Tails questioned, still rubbing her arm. Having fingerprints all over her body was equally as bad as having hives. She glanced at her nails. They'd need to be trimmed before she scratched sores in her flesh.

"His name is Brodie," Zeus said, flashing a smile of satisfaction. "He needs a get-out-of-jail-free card and fast. Then he must attend the next session at the community centre. I've found a replacement for Dejardins that no one will question."

"How am I supposed to help this Brodie, exactly?" Tails complained. "I have no idea how to get him where you want him."

"Really, Tails," he said. "You know exactly how. Use your God-given gifts. You never had any problem doing that before. Besides, it's Judge Hawethorne. We all know he's the biggest pervert on the bench. Use some of your bushy tails."

She turned her head away. The stinging in her eyes showed a weakness no man deserved to see. "And if I refuse?" she croaked.

Zeus exhaled briskly. "There is no room for a conscience in a revolution," he replied. "Don't fill your pretty head with visions of settling down in the countryside. We both know that isn't who you are." He paused. "And what you are good at."

Her head snapped back. "I'm not some play toy you can toss to whoever you want! I can serve the purpose in other ways."

Zeus chuckled. "Of course you could," he admitted. "But, frankly, what we need you the most for is your seductive powers." He raised a finger in the air. "Do this job and it will be the last time I ask you to perform such a task."

"I have your word?" Tails asked.

"Foxes' honour," Zeus replied, making a cross over his heart.

# Chapter Five

Brodie shuffled into to courtroom. Even with the added balance all shifters possessed, walking wasn't easy in leg irons. A wooden gate swung back, hitting his knees. They bent, accepting pain as an added punishment. Any yelp could have been construed as aggression. If what Gerald told him was even partly true, he needed to keep all emotions under wraps.

A guard pushed him down in a chair, attaching his handcuffs to a metal plate on the table. He could stand, but go no farther. He glanced over his shoulder. There wasn't a protester in sight. In fact, the room was completely empty except for himself and three guards. It made sense. No one was concerned about what happened to a good-for-nothing shifter. If they were, there was bound to be several trials later in the day they could catch with exactly the same results.

The attorneys strolled in, arguing between themselves in no more than a whisper. Brodie chuckled under his breath. Lowering one's voice didn't make their behaviour any less a quarrel. Disagreements were the basis of everyday life. How ironic that he was being charged because he had a dispute of his own.

Gerald shook his head, taking his place beside his client. "Looks like we are going to have to do this the hard way. The prosecutor's office is refusing to deal."

The words registered in Brodie's mind, but held little meaning. The drugs had kicked in, leaving him with a nonchalant demeanour. Time diminished to barely a crawl, everything moving in slow motion. Even his lawyer's words seemed to take forever to fully form. There was a zero percent chance he'd be trying to make his own sentences anytime soon.

"All rise," a guard bellowed.

Gerald grabbed Brodie's arm and tugged him to his feet.

"The Honourable Judge Hawethorne proceeding," the guard continued.

Brodie strained to clear the fogginess of his vision. He wanted to see the man who was about to convict him of the crime of existence. The problem was he couldn't be sure his eyes were doing their job correctly. If they were, the man presiding over the court appeared to be a middle-aged, overweight vampire wannabe. Of course, there were also fairies dancing around his gavel, too. He picked the worst time to go on a bad trip. The tiny hammer rose in the air and came smashing down on the heads of at least two of the tiny winged women. Try as he might, he couldn't avoid flinching at the sight of their squashed bodies.

"Be seated," Judge Hawethorne ordered. "Let's get this over in a timely fashion, shall we? I'll hear from the prosecutor."

The opposing lawyer stood to present his case. There wasn't much he needed to say, other than in directing the judge as to where in the paperwork he could find the evidence that had been fabricated and stacked against the defendant.

"All right," Judge Hawethorne said. "I think I've heard all I need to. This seems like an open-and-shut case. I see no reason to waste anymore of our taxpayers' hard earned money on it."

"Your honour!" Gerald exclaimed. "This is highly unusual. I haven't had an opportunity to present a defence as of yet. Surely you aren't considering judgment without disclosure from both sides?"

Fumes rose from behind the bench, rage bubbling under the judge's skin. "Are you questioning the court?!" he bellowed.

"It is my job to question the court if I am not allowed to properly defend a client," Gerald answered. His fingers locked together between his back.

"I would hardly call this shifter a client," the judge scoffed. "Having a defence is a privilege; one that isn't meant for animals. I've already made my decision and nothing you or anyone else can say will alter..."

The door at the back of the room swung open, allowing the clicking of high heels on the tile floor through. Brodie inhaled a sweet floral scent, instantly recognizing it. His mind began to clear, focusing on the woman he'd almost met once before. A simple glance over his shoulder placed him directly into a web of smouldering sexuality. She wore the equivalent of a little black dress—except in all white—and it left little to the imagination. Even so, he and every other man in the room would have given both their arms and legs to have a peek underneath it. The rest of her was shrouded in mystery, from oversized sunglasses to a wide-brimmed hat.

Why she covered up her luscious locks was beyond him. Her hair was by far her best feature, especially the highlights.

From the moment he noticed it the previous night, a desire had burned within him to run his fingers through it, taking stock of each and every colour, strand by strand.

"We'll take a quick recess," Judge Hawethorne said, loosening his tie. He whispered in the ear of the nearest guard to escort the strange woman back to his chambers.

Her lips curled up at the edges as she passed him by. Once again Brodie's voice failed and he was left watching her backside leave him behind.

"What just happened?" Brodie asked.

"I'm not sure," Gerald answered. "Do you know that woman?"

Brodie considered his options, exchanging glances between the two lawyers. The last thing he needed was to blurt out some information that might provide the prosecutor with a new angle to use in the case against him. "No," he replied. "I don't know her." Technically it wasn't a lie. She had been present at the incident, but if the lawyers working this case didn't know who she was, he wasn't going to tell them.

"Maybe she's a relative," the prosecutor suggested, twirling a pen between his fingers. It fell, rolling from the desk to the floor.

"I don't think anyone believes that woman is his long-lost cousin," Gerald snickered. "Whoever she is, hopefully she can put him in a better mood."

"You've already lost," the prosecutor scoffed. "Waiting for the sentence is merely a formality and we both know it."

# Chapter Six

Brodie's eyes fixed on the chamber entrance, waiting for it to open and reveal whatever secrets lay hidden behind the heavy oak door. The mystery woman wasn't anywhere near him, and yet her allure teased him. Thoughts of what she might have been doing with the judge in private brought his blood to its boiling point. As his blood pressure rose, so did his frustration.

Whatever concoction Gerald forced on him had done the trick, but was wearing thin. Brodie craved another dose. A growl formed in his throat at his own weakness, masked only by his own breath. A mere taste of emotion control medication had left him feeling like a seasoned junkie. The last of his nerves were on edge. A crack echoed through the otherwise silent court. His neck twisted to the side, hoping to relieve building tension. All attempts failed. The mounting pressure had all the aggravation of an itch he couldn't scratch.

There were no clocks on the walls, nor watch on his wrist. It didn't matter. His internal hourglass had that covered. They had been twiddling their thumbs for over an hour, waiting for the judge to return. Even the prosecuting attorney was beginning to grow weary, slouching back in his chair and glancing at the ceiling fan as it completed one cycle after another. There was little else to occupy the mind. Perhaps that was part of the game. Leaving the pot to see how long it would take to boil over—a watched pot never did—after all. Brodie wasn't playing, though, at least not yet. He could take a bit more torture before giving up. The court officers were the ones who deserved being pitied. They remained as still as a queen's guards did while protecting the palace. That couldn't have been easy.

Brodie's attention turned to his own discomfort; dry tongue feeling around his teeth, seeking out what little moisture remained. It smacked against the roof of his mouth. The whole process was as futile as trying to swallow in a dentist's chair, the mini vacuum sucking up all the saliva. He eyed a pitcher of water. Condensation ran down the crystal clear sides, taunting him as ice within melted. He longed for a single sip, but knew it wasn't placed there for the enjoyment of the accused. Gerald poured a couple of mouthfuls into a glass cup.

"What are you doing?" the prosecutor complained. "That water isn't for the likes of him. It was put here for the professionals forced to endure a long day because of his kind. I object to you serving criminals."

"Save your objections for the judge," Gerald huffed. "It's a glass of water, not one of the expensive fruity drinks you enjoy. How big is your tiny umbrella collection?"

"Very funny," the prosecutor groaned. "I'll report you if his lips contaminate that glass. I, for one, wouldn't want to have to drink from it after. The thought of an animal's saliva all over it makes me queasy."

"They do wash them," Gerald blurted out.

"That doesn't get rid of all the germs," the prosecutor argued. "Who knows what's been in his filthy mouth. There are bowls on the floor in the hallway. He can wait."

"Sorry," Gerald muttered, replacing the glass.

Brodie grasped his shoulder attempting to stop his arm from shaking. His stomach ached in turmoil. A cold sweat formed on his brow.

Gerald offered a swift pat on the back. "It'll all be over soon," he said, smiling in the direction of the prosecutor.

Life crept back into the room, bodies perking up at the first sign of movement from the judge's quarters. The mystery woman appeared first, looking no worse for wear. Her tongue darted out, licking plump red lips as she passed him by on her way out.

Brodie blinked, his vision clouded by a rose-coloured fog. Every muscle relaxed; frustration melting away. His own inner turmoil was far too much energy to waste. A numbness took over his body, spreading from head to toe, before seeping into the depths of his mind.

His gaze veered to meet his lawyer's. It was a bold move to drug a shifter in a courtroom. If Gerald had been caught, he would have found himself on the chopping block as well. By the time Brodie turned back, the mystery woman had vanished; the clicking of her heels the only proof left she had ever been there. Even those were becoming nothing more than a faint memory.

"I'm back," Judge Hawethorne declared, a smile etched on his face from ear to ear. "Where were we? Ah, yes. I've received some last minute evidence that I have decided to take into consideration."

"Evidence," the prosecutor complained, "what evidence? I have a right to full disclosure of anything that has bearing on the case."

"You have the right to what I say you have the right to," the judge argued, banging a wooden gavel on its stand several times. "This court orders: the accused shall go back to anger management classes for a full threat evaluation. The results of that assessment will determine whether or not further sentencing is necessary. This court will reconvene in thirty days." He banged the gavel one more time with force.

"What just happened?" Brodie whispered to his attorney.

"I'm not sure," Gerald replied. The smile creeping up the sides of his face made contact with his long bushy sideburns. "Who is the broad?"

"I don't know her," Brodie replied.

"Right," Gerald snickered, elbowing his client. "I wasn't born yesterday. Beautiful women don't normally show up in a courtroom and offer their services to save a total stranger."

"You think he went easy on me because of her?" Brodie asked, his brow arched. He shook his head. None of it made any sense.

"I know it was because of her," Gerald replied. "Judge Hawthorne was about to throw the book at you. Don't take it personally; he's one of the biggest supporters of the Human Rights Movement. He goes hard on all shifters."

Brodie didn't answer. There was more on his mind than a corrupt judge with a bad case of shifter hate. He tore through the possibilities as to why anyone would want to come to his aid. Love at first sight didn't exist; he had no useful information to protect; he wasn't a spy or even in a well paying job; and he didn't have any real assets. His life was boring, at best, a routine that was cringe worthy.

"Earth to Brodie," Gerald called out, waving a hand before his client's face, "are you listening to me?"

"Sorry, what?" Brodie asked.

"It's time to go," Gerald answered. "Unless you'd like to wait for a different judge to come in and reverse the decision."

Brodie glanced down at his hands. The cuffs had already been removed. He shook his head. "No, of course not. I was..."

"Trying to remember where you met the girl?" Gerald suggested. "She was something. If you figure it out, let me know. I wouldn't mind getting a hold of her number." He cleared his throat. "For professional reasons... to help out my other clients, of course."

"Can't help, sorry," Brodie said. "I have no idea how to contact her myself."

"That's a shame," Gerald said, holding the door open. "I'll give you a ride home. I am sure I don't need to tell you that you have to attend every session of the class, or you'll be in contempt of court."

"And yet you did tell me," Brodie blurted out. "Thanks for the vote of confidence. I think I'll walk. Have a good day, Gerald."

"Check in with me," Gerald called after him.

Brodie waved one hand over his head without looking back. He wasn't about to miss a class when that was his only connection to the mysterious woman. He also didn't plan on sharing that information with his attorney.

# Chapter Seven

Brodie stood at the top of the stairs near the entrance, hoping to catch his mystery woman before entering. The hands on his wristwatch begged him to give up. The hour was late and soon he would be, too. A shaky hand fumbled around for change in his front pocket, retrieving what it could find. His sweaty palm held out just enough to buy a drink. A finger pushed the single coin around hoping it might magically transform into two. It didn't.

*Damn!*

He smacked his forehead with his free hand. Not bringing money for a second time was an oversight that shouldn't have been made. He remembered to grab the one coin, but that was to replay the foxy lady with. A moocher wasn't the first impression he hoped to make. It didn't reflect who he was. His debts were always paid on time and in full. It wasn't as if he couldn't afford to. There was cash, maybe not a lot of it in comparison to the rich and famous, but some nonetheless. He just left it sitting on his bedside table. The coin flipped in the air. Heads, he used it for a drink, and tails, he'd wait it out and return it if the mystery lady appeared. That was a fair way to decide. She'd even been the one to call it the previous week— tails. Apparently, it always won. Looking down at his wrist, he let out a hefty chuckle. She was right. Strutting by the machine without so much as a glance back, he headed for the door. The coin belonged to her. Tails was victorious.

Brodie eyed the guards stationed outside the meeting room, wondering if their increase in proximity had anything to do with him. His glance alternated between stern faces, held perfectly still. He nodded at each as he passed. The gesture, however, went unanswered.

Dejardins, as Gerald had called him, looked exactly the same as the first time Brodie had laid eyes on him. His knees trembled for the first few steps. That was a bad case of overthinking. Worrying about what would come to pass when their vision connected wasn't helping. In the best scenario, the man had met enough other troublemakers that he wouldn't remember one face from another. It was also the least likely. He cleared the building lump from his throat. The muffled half-cough garnered attention.

Dejardins tossed his glasses aside, looking up. His eyes narrowed as he scrutinized the newest member to his program. "I trust we won't be having any problems with you this evening," he said.

"No, sir," Brodie answered.

"Good," Dejardins snorted. "Take a seat. Keep your eyes on the ground. I don't want to hear a peep out of you for the entire meeting." His brown eyes turned black. If anyone needed anger management it was him. Brodie mulled over his option. Dejardins was already annoyed at his existence, adding to that was a bad idea.

The room was set up poorly to accomplish class goals. If anything it leaned more toward a shifter torture chamber than a place for them to safely learn to control their tempers. The colour scheme itself brought the primal side of one's nature to the forefront. There was a reason why bullfighters carried red capes. The shade enraged the beast side of the animals.

If that wasn't bad enough, there was the matter of the chairs. They were too small to comfortably fit almost any fully-grown man and woman. Their plastic bottoms curved, forcing the spine into an unnatural form. Still, those in attendance were tasked with picking one to endure for the evening.

In general, Brodie's choices were rarely good ones. His ability to end up in the only line at the grocery store that didn't budge was uncanny. That talent proved true once again. The moment he put any weight on the seat, it cracked its disapproval at being chosen loudly.

Brodie grimaced at the noise; his eyes glued shut. He didn't need to see to know all the other attendees were glaring in his direction. Everyone heard the snapping noise. That made things even more difficult. If he stayed put, he ran the chance that the chair was probably going to give out, sending him crashing to the floor. Moving to another made him out to be a jerk, leaving a chair that could collapse open for some other schmuck to try their luck in. In the end, chancing the accident won the battle, being a smidge better than being labelled an a-hole.

Brodie's weight shifted, putting less pressure on the middle of the plastic. That didn't help. If anything it made things worse. Not only was the plastic groaning, but he could also hear the snickers of his fellow anger management classmates. Who could blame them, though? He was a sight to see: beet red face and butt lifted off the chair on one side. The exact same mannerisms of a constipated man trying to sneak a fart through clogged pipes on his throne.

Of course, it was inevitable that she would walk in at precisely that moment. She paused, pulling her sunglasses down to allow a short glimpse of her playful eyes glancing him over. Her lips parted slightly, before the glasses returned to their rightful position, and she took a seat on the opposite side of the room.

There was never a second opportunity to make a first impression. Then again, technically this wasn't their first time meeting, not that it helped the situation any. Brodie struggled, not being able to lift his gaze to her face. It was even harder restraining himself from charging up to her and grabbing a fistful of her flowing locks. The sweet scent her hair emitted should have been considered a drug. One whiff and he had been instantly addicted. The worst part about it was he hadn't even realized how much he'd been craving her.

Brodie's pants tightened; he shifted; the chair cracked. It was a never-ending cycle of humiliation. A stolen glimpse confirmed his suspicions. Even if the room was silent, there was laughter in her eyes. His heartbeat increased, blood rushing to his face, keeping it crimson.

Brodie's gaze locked on the floor in front of him again. He concentrated on his shoelaces, one being on the verge of becoming untied. He didn't dare fix it, though. That would have drawn even more scrutiny in his direction, not to mention the ire of the one in charge. Instead, he let the string consume his thoughts, contemplating the best possible way for it to be retied. A shoelace couldn't judge him or his decisions. The droplets of sweat, that had threatened to form on his brow, all but dried up the moment his pulse and breathing returned to normal.

Dejardins had made it clear; no words were to be uttered under any circumstances. Instead of his vocal chords, Brodie's toes celebrated for him. They wiggled within the confines of the shoes, laughing from a place that was hidden from view. It was ironic in a way. Dejardins hadn't planned on actually teaching them anything, but he managed to learn something from him anyway. Lesson one was complete. Concentrating on an object outside conflict was a form of emotional control.

# Chapter Eight

Silence was darkness to the ears and every bit as eerie and frightening, carrying with it the same message of despair. A pit of nothingness engulfed him, enticing emotions that had been locked deep away in his soul to bubble on the surface. Anything with a power great enough to mute Mother Nature deserved his fear.

The sound of trees rustling in the wind; the sweet call of a bird to its mate; they were things Brodie took for granted. That was a mistake that never should have been made. Without them, the picture wasn't complete. It was a masterpiece, waiting for its defining finishing touches to be added. Hearing was a gift to be cherished. It deserved the proper admiration and attention other senses received.

He inhaled. Even the sound of his own breath was missing. The air froze as it passed through his lips again. The cloud it formed drifted off into the background, disappearing somewhere between himself and the skyline. That was the first clue it was cold.

Brodie glanced down, toes wiggling back at him their concern. The fresh layer of snow beneath them should have melted on contact, yet somehow it remained intact. The sensation of feeling the crunch beneath his feet, but not being able to hear it amused him. A chuckle attempted an escape from its prison, but failed. He could feel the struggle building in his throat. Laughter lost the battle, conceding its defeat to the new ruler of the roost, pain. He grasped at his neck, feeling the ache spreading like wildfires. Saliva glands were the last defence against further damage. They put up a valiant effort, but in the end, the hoses ran dry. An unquenchable thirst joined the party.

The first snowflake to fall caught on his eyelashes. He blinked it free, a grin forming over ravenous lips. He opened the palm of his hand, catching a few more, before allowing his tongue to play the game as well. Moisture slowly returned to his mouth and throat. It was a piece of heaven in the middle of the fiery pits of hell.

Brodie spun around, arms outstretched, head tilted back and mouth wide open, catching as many of the flakes as he could. Every drop soothed his anguish a smidge more. A handful of the cold powder lifted to his mouth. His tongue reached out, lapping at his palm for every taste.

Brodie's grin vanished. He glared at the red stripes left behind on his hand. Fingers reached for his lips, coming back covered in the same ruby liquid. His lips quivered in time with shaking knees. Red dots appeared on the white surface around him. The heavens opened up and blood rained down, covering his clothes, skin, and hair.

He'd tasted blood and all he wanted was more.

****

Brodie bolted up right in his bed, saturated in sweat. Every muscle tensed, poised to attack at a moment's notice. "It was a dream," he repeated several times over amidst bated breath. "It was only a dream." He flopped backward, head hitting a pillow. One hand glided over his bare chest, checking for blood. There was none. He inhaled and exhaled deeply several times over. His heart rate slowly returned back to a normal rhythm.

It had been years since nightmares had plagued his sleep. A trigger had been pulled, releasing his worst fears back into his subconscious. It wasn't the only thing that returned, though. A single memory hitched a ride, piggybacking on the terror that was born in a child's mind.

His mother's voice sang a sweet lullaby to ease her son into slumber. The words eluded him, but the melody was undeniable. Every note had been manufactured with one purpose in mind; removing the anxiety everyday life created and replacing it with hope of a better day to come.

He stole a glance at the alarm clock. There were still a few hours before he needed to be up. It didn't matter, though. There was no hope for further sleep that evening, especially alone in a room that would never be a real home.

Brodie longed to find that one special person who could soothe his soul in the same manner his mother had. In his mind, that wasn't a lot to ask of life, the teeniest bit of happiness. It wasn't as if he expected anyone to take all his problems away. All he wanted was to find someone he could sleep soundly through the night beside, even amidst the craziness that was bound to continue to happen.

# Chapter Nine

When it came to grooming, only some people had talent. Brodie's hair had a mind of its own. The longer he stood in front of a mirror combing it, the more defiant it became. Natural curls formed kinks that brought back memories of his teen years. Even the strongest members of a flock experienced growing pains. He lacked the support a pack of his own would have provided, that made being accepted by others a necessity. It was difficult enough dealing with the constant inner battle between his two halves, without worrying about teenage drama as well.

Every hair style he tried failed, still he ventured on, searching for the one that someone, other than himself, thought was cool. Finally, he gave up and decided to simply let it grow. A little bit of conditioner and a hair tie had been all he needed until then.

Brodie tilted his head from side to side, eyeing the image in the mirror. His head shook. Pushing thirty and a beautiful woman only had to smile his way to tie his insides in knots; pathetic was the term that came to mind. Now that the spiffing up ritual had begun, there was no choice but to see it through.

The brush submerged under flowing water from the tap, wetting it thoroughly. He slicked back his hair, hoping to erase all the damage his previous efforts caused. A curl popped up, frizzing out to mock his latest attempt, its close friends joined it. If he let it dry completely, he'd end up looking like he stuck a finger in an electrical socket at best. A full shower was the only way to rectify the situation. This time he'd leave styling out of the equation.

His fingers tugged at a few the bristles forming on his chin. They weren't quite worthy of a full shave. One of the downfalls of being a male shifter was the amount of time it took to grow facial hair, especially for those who preferred the clean-shaven look. The beard phase of his life had come and gone in one season. It simply didn't suit his features.

Baring teeth, Brodie snarled and growled at his own reflection. That was the only preparation that could be made for spending an entire evening in silence. A sigh escaped slightly parted lips at the thought of the mystery woman. It was hard for a male peacock to impress a female if it wasn't allowed to dance.

The watch on his wrist beeped. It was time to leave for the meeting. He cracked his knuckles before slinging a jacket over his shoulder and heading out the door.

*****

The night air was eerily still and absent of all odours. A nervous electricity sparked between his fingers. *The calm before the storm.*

He glanced up at a full moon, partly hidden by clouds. Its natural glow had been replaced by a faint crimson colour. *A blood moon.*

The forecast for the evening was grim at best. The moon's normal cycles held little sway over shifters. It was the rare occurrences that they had to watch out for. Eclipses and colour changes fired up the beast dwelling inside. He swallowed back his own animal instincts to flee. Even if there had been a choice, it was too late. He was already standing outside the building and it was as dark and ominous as the night air.

He mustered his courage, inhaling deeply, before climbing the steps, taking them one at a time. One hand shoved into a pocket while the other pulled open the door. His fingers fumbled with a sole coin, the one he had yet to return. There hadn't been the opportunity before. Tonight was going to be different.

The security guards paid the same amount of attention to him as they did his previous visit; which amounted to none. He scooted by them heading straight for his creaky chair.

"Sign in!" the old man running the show demanded.

Brodie turned to comply, glancing up for only a brief moment to acknowledge the request. His head snapped back, hoping for a second glimpse of a flash of yellow and green in Dejardins' eyes. If it had been there, it was gone. The ominous feeling it brought with it, however, remained. He took his seat, noticing there wasn't a single creak or crack to be heard. It had been fixed or swapped.

"I think we are all here," Dejardins said. "Let's begin, shall we? Tonight we will be analyzing your negative reactions to different situations. I want you to tear them apart until you uncover an equally satisfying approach lying underneath, one that fosters no resentment or anger. Each of you will need to listen to this." He passed out a pair of headphones to every member of the circle, before nodding to the mystery woman. "Put them on. Hurry!"

The attendees all followed the instructions. Brodie scrambled, shoving one in each ear, while watching Dejardins and the woman furiously typing on the teacher's laptop. They were up to something. He was sure of it—even more so when they pushed tiny buds into their own ears as well—using some form of sign language to communicate.

Brodie concentrated on the woman's hands, trying to make out a word or two and wishing he'd taken a special course on signing. Her mouth moved, but lip-reading wasn't one of his talents either. Attempts to figure out what was going on were abruptly interrupted. The two guards rushed in, freezing just inside the doorway. Their faces contorted, hands reaching to cover their ears. They fell to their knees in sync, passing out on the floor.

Dejardins motioned with one hand for the group to follow them into the hallway. Gone were the movements of an old man, replaced by the agility of a trained ninja. Leading the group to stairs heading down, he took two steps at a time, sometimes three, in a race to the bottom. Once there, a few raps on a wall opened a secret passageway. He ushered them all in, before collecting the ear pieces.

"Welcome to the revolution," the woman announced. "Head to your right. There is transportation waiting to take you to freedom and a better life to come."

# Chapter Ten

Joining a revolution was the furthest possible thought from Brodie's mind when he woke up that day, and it still wasn't anywhere near his top ten things to do. From the faces of the others, he gathered each of them felt the same way. None of them had been honestly recruited. This was a forceful draft.

There was a level of concern escalating rapidly in the back of the white cube truck that had been loosely referred to as transportation. A bus might have been better than herding a group of civilians into the back of a produce carrier without anything to hold onto. They weren't even afforded an access to fresh air that slaughter animals were en route.

Every turn the driver took had them stumbling around, whacking into each other and walls. If the ride became any bumpier, their kidnappers were in for an outright riot. No one in their group was a mercenary for hire or even trained militia.

They might have all been shifters, but that didn't mean they knew how to fight, or even act, being thrown into a strange environment.

A sharp turn knocked the group to one side, bodies flying. Brodie staggered, trying to keep his balance. A woman screamed, her knees buckling. He reached out, snatching her out of the path of being crushed by a muscular man, mid shift. Tension was rising. Packing a volatile group into small quarters was crazy enough, but adding the element of danger was a huge mistake.

A thought crossed Brodie's mind. Maybe it was all part of the test. Whoever was in charge was trying to provoke a response, using the most stressful situations they could come up with. That had to be it. To pass all he had to do was stay calm. Of course, that was easier said than done.

The truck jerked to a stop. The doors opened, a stampede to exit ensued. After that horrific ride, anything was an improvement. He ate his own words at the first sight of the dreary narrow corridor they were herded down. Dejardins was nowhere to be seen. The mysterious woman had taken control, ushering them in pairs into separate, yet identical, rooms containing a single dresser and a set of bunk beds.

"This will be your new home," the woman bellowed. "You will be fed, clothed, and taken care of. In return, each of you will be required to do your part in the battle for equality." She motioned for the final couple in front of him to head into their living quarters.

Brodie bit his tongue for as long as he could. "Excuse me," he whispered in the least threatening way possible.

The woman turned. "What is it?" she snapped, her hands placed firmly on either hip. One foot tapped on the concrete floor.

"I think there has been a mistake," Brodie suggested.

"Again with the mistake," she mocked. "That line didn't do much for you last time you used it. You should learn from your mistakes."

"Probably," Brodie admitted. "It's just I'm not really militia material. I don't think violence is the answer to all problems."

"Let me guess, you're a lover not a fighter," the woman scoffed.

"Pretty much," Brodie agreed. "Except I'm not really good at either." He let out a huff. "This would be a lot easier if I at least knew your name."

"I'm hurt you forgot my name so easily," she said, a scowl forming over her otherwise wrinkle-free complexion. "That doesn't happen often." She turned, hiding a smile.

"I would remember if you told me," Brodie argued. "That reminds me." His hand dove into his front pocket, retrieving a shiny coin. "This belongs to you." He tossed it in the air.

The woman caught it in a tightly clenched fist. "I'll tell you what. Call it. If you are right, I'll tell you my name."

"You seem to like tails," Brodie said. "So I guess I'll take heads." A coy smile crossed his lips, rewarding him for his own wittiness.

A cheeky smile graced her face. "Never bet against tails," she teased, tongue darting out to leave a layer of moisture in the place of lipstick. Her hand opened; eyes never once straying from his.

He blinked first. A quick glimpse confirmed she was right. "How did you know?" he asked. "Statistically speaking there is a fifty percent chance of it being heads. Winning every time is an impossibility."

"Want to try again?" she mocked.

The coin flew up in the air once more. This time he caught it, flipping it upside down on the back of his hand.

"Go on," the woman ordered, "take a look. I dare you."

He licked his lips, his hand slowly moving away. The shiny circle mocked him for ever trying. "Two out of three," he begged, the coin already mid-flight.

She leaned against the wall, lips pursed together in a told-you-so fashion. "You plan on flipping that coin all day?" she jested adding, a chuckle to the end of her words.

"I'm telling you it is impossible for it to always be tails," Brodie whined. He checked both sides to make sure the coin hadn't been tampered with. "What am I missing?"

"The obvious," the woman replied. "This way."

"Don't I get a fancy room?" Brodie scoffed. "I thought we might be bunkies."

"Sorry to disappoint, but the boss wants to see you," she replied. "He seems to think there is something special about you. I haven't figured out what, yet. Maybe it's your shifted form. What is it, anyway?"

"I don't shift," Brodie answered, his face cold and stern. That was one decision from his past he had no intentions of wavering on for anyone.

She stopped and glanced over her shoulder at him. "You are a shifter, right?"

"I guess," Brodie answered. "It isn't that big a deal. It's not like we can change into our other form whenever we want. The humans don't allow it... in case you forgot."

"Trust me, I didn't," she blurted out. "That's what this place is all about. We want to change things. We want to be treated as equals. I've been fighting for it my whole life. One day we'll be able to live our lives without hiding from the rest of society."

"So what type of shifter are you?" Brodie asked.

"A fox," she answered.

A grin crept over his face. "That makes sense... 'cause you are one foxy lady." His mouth shut tight, instantly regretting the words it had just spewed out.

"Like I haven't heard that one before," she mused. "You really should work on your pick-up lines. That was pathetic. We're here." She opened a door leading to an almost completely empty club.

Brodie glanced around, his sharp eyesight locking on a middle-aged man. "Who is that?" he asked. "I feel as if I've seen him before."

"That's Zeus," she replied. "He runs the place."

"And finances it," Zeus commented as they drew near. "Thank you, Tails, I'll take it from here. Pour yourself a drink and find something to occupy your time."

"Tails," he muttered, chuckling under his breath. That crossed off a few questions on his list. It still didn't explain the coin always landing tails side up, though.

"I'll take a pass on the spirits. You should, too. It's a little early for drinking. Don't you think?" Tails complained.

"When you are in charge, you can do as you please," Zeus scoffed. "For the moment, however, I am the one leading the show. That means I decide when the bar opens, my dear. Off you go." He made a shooing motion with his hands. "That's right."

Brodie watched her comply with out any resistance. The strong woman he'd met simply melted away to one man's voice. "Is she..."

"No," Zeus said, chuckling. "At least, not in the way you are thinking. I own her, but she's no one's mate. That includes you. I don't mind if you play with her, of course. That's part of the perks of signing up."

"I haven't signed up for anything," Brodie snapped. "And I don't think Tails would appreciate you talking about her like that."

"Tails knows her place," Zeus groaned. "We all have jobs to do for the cause. Hers is simply being a whore."

"What?!" Brodie exclaimed.

"Well, how did you think she got you a get out of jail free card?" Zeus questioned, his brows arched. "She used her assets, of course. You didn't actually believe she said pretty please, did you?" He chuckled. "Or perhaps you thought she got down on her knees and begged for your forgiveness. Then again she might have been on all fours..."

Brodie licked his lips, shaking his head. His vision never faltered from her, as she swayed back and forth to some soft music playing in the background. The idea of the judge's hands all over that body gnawed at his insides. His primal nature screamed, demanding to be released. Beads of sweat formed on his brow.

"It's okay." Zeus placed an arm around Brodie's shoulders. Squeezing tightly, he continued, "It's totally normal to feel an intense interest in Tails. Most men do. That's what makes her good at the tasks she is given. Feel free to have some fun... just remember that there won't be a white wedding and a happy wife at the end of the day."

"What is it you want from me?" Brodie asked.

"I want you to join the cause," Zeus explained. "That's all. I want you to come and be my right-hand man."

"And if I refuse?" Brodie asked. "What if I want to go back to a normal life?"

"A normal life?" Zeus scoffed. "What sort of a life do you think you can have? If you leave here, you'll end up back in prison, this time on death row."

"I didn't do anything, though," Brodie complained.

"I know," Zeus replied, shaking his head. "It's a huge injustice, but I'm afraid they already found Dejardins' body. They know a shifter killed him. Guess who was the last one to have an argument with him."

Brodie pointed to his own chest.

"That's right," Zeus said. "You already know they won't even give you an opportunity to open your mouth in defence. That's what we are trying to change and you can help."

"There were others who saw him," Brodie argued.

"The others saw a substitute," Zeus explained. "He was already dead by then. No one is coming to your rescue if you end up on the wrong side of the law this time."

"That's blackmail!" Brodie exclaimed.

"I prefer to call it business," Zeus replied. "Why don't you sleep on it and we'll talk again tomorrow?" He lifted a silver bell.

"You rang," Tails said, returning.

"Take our guest to a comfortable suite and then return," Zeus ordered. "I have a few odds and ends for you to tie up this evening."

# Chapter Eleven

"You can't stay mad forever," Tails complained, leading the way up a winding set of stairs. Her hand glided over the railing, admiring the curve of the wood rather than using it as an aid.

"Why can't I?" Brodie blurted back. "I've been kidnapped, held against my will, framed for murder, and blackmailed... all in one day. In case you didn't know, that's a new record for me."

"You left out rescued," Tails argued.

Brodie huffed, forcing his bangs to lift and fall. "That sort of rescue I can do without," he scoffed. "My lawyer had it under control."

Your lawyer is an idiot!" Tails exclaimed. "If you can't see that he's on the pay, you're an even bigger one. If I hadn't shown up, you would have been locked up for life. Thank your lucky stars Zeus had need of you."

"Yeah, about that," Brodie snarled, "How exactly did you change the judge's mind? Did you just ask him nicely?"

"Did Zeus suggest otherwise?" she asked, stopping on a landing to glance back at him. "I guess it doesn't matter. You are going to believe whatever you want. I can't change that." Without waiting for a response, the climb began again.

Silence created a divide between them. It wasn't the normal awkward that caused boy likes girl verbal loss. This was a deeper divide. Their relationship was still in the sheet of glass stage: fragile. In the past few minutes a hairline crack had formed. Harsh words accelerated the fracturing process. New branches splintered off with every word uttered. A few too many and it would shatter, wounding them both. The chances of reversing the process were slim to none. Still, he decided to try, swallowing his own pride in the process. Tails brought out a part of him he thought had been lost with his parents, years ago.

"This is your room," Tails stated, pointing to the first door on the left. "I'm down the hall on the left."

"I'm sorry," Brodie whispered in her ear as he passed.

Her heartbeat purred a song; one that was normally reserved for mothers humming to their children at bedtime and lovers embracing under twinkling stars. Those two words were more than anyone had bothered to say to her in an extremely long time. It was more than that, though. There was more to Brodie. Even with his rough exterior, an air of royalty surrounded him, strong enough to make her want to bow down before him when he entered a room. She hadn't yet put her finger on what Zeus wanted him for, but she was getting closer to finding out.

"Why don't you shift?" Tails questioned. "You never did answer me before."

"It's a long story," Brodie answered, averting his gaze from hers. "If you stay with me tonight, I'll tell it to you."

Her eyes widened.

"Just to talk," Brodie blurted out. "I wasn't thinking..."

"To talk," Tails repeated, entering the room. "I'll stay until you fall asleep, but then I have to go."

"Thanks." Brodie took a seat on the floor beside her. "It's strange being here. I'm not sure I could ever get used to this place."

Tails offered a sympathetic smile. "I suppose I am used to it," she admitted. "I've been here since I was a young girl."

"What about your parents?" Brodie asked.

Tails took in a deep breath and huffed it out quickly. "My mother was caught by the government, back when shifters were first discovered. They used her as a test subject in crossbreeding experiments. My father was nothing more than an unknown sperm donor."

"I'm sorry," Brodie muttered. "Those were brutal times."

"It isn't much better now," Tails replied. "I was the runt of a litter of five. Over the years we were held captive, they took my siblings one by one, running tests on each until their last breath expired. I was the only one remaining. When my mother saw a chance to escape, she grabbed me and ran. They chased us, of course, but we kept evading them at every corner. That's when she took ill. A doctor was out of the question. They would have turned us in without treatment anyway."

"I thought doctors remained neutral at all times," Brodie said. "It's supposed to be part of their oath or something."

Tails chuckled. "That's what they tell people, but it isn't true. It's a bit better now, but back then, any shifter on the street knew the horrors that awaited them in medical care. It often was a fate far worse than the military's experimentation."

"So how did you get away?" Brodie asked.

"There was word on the street about a club that was friendly to our kind," Tails explained. "We took a chance. That's how I ended up here. Zeus agreed to take me in and protect me."

"And your mother?" Brodie asked.

"She was very ill," Tails said. "She wasn't going to make it. Her captors had implanted trackers deep in her organs that no one could ever remove. If she stayed, armed forces would have located Zeus's operation and come in guns blazing. He couldn't let that happen and neither could she."

"She sacrificed herself for you," Brodie mumbled.

"I was heartbroken, of course," Tails said. "I was too young to understand back then." She sniffled and chuckled at the same time. "I don't think I ate or spoke for a month."

"How did you get over it?" Brodie asked.

"I didn't," Tails answered. "I don't think anyone can ever fully get over something like that. Things changed, though. The world kept turning. Zeus started my training as one of his operatives in the fight for shifter rights. That became my life...

my purpose." She crossed her legs, shuffling to face him. "I've told you my story. Your turn."

"I began the change early, at the age of eight," Brodie explained.

"That's extremely young," Tails blurted out.

"Yeah," Brodie admitted. "Too young. I couldn't control it. My parents took me to specialists who were friends of the family and trusted. No one could figure out what was happening to me. I guess those trips set off an alarm somewhere. I woke up one night in my mother's arms, racing for the car. I remember looking over her shoulder at our burning house and crying."

"The army?" Tails questioned.

Brodie shook his head. "My father started it. For an eight-year-old it was more frightening than a nightmare. Even worse for me, being afraid made the shifts start. They fastened me in the back of the car, but the changing forms rendered the seat belt useless. My father didn't slow down, though. I don't even know who we were running from. That's when I did my first full shift. I could see horror in my father's eyes in the rear-view mirror. My mother turned around and gasped. There was a loud crash and everything went black. When I woke up I was lying in a bed of freshly fallen snow. The car was destroyed, my parents dead. That's why I can't ever shift again. Whatever I am, it killed my parents. I am responsible." A tear ran down his cheek.

"You don't know that," Tails said, her hand on his shoulder. "Do you remember anything else from that night?"

"Not much," Brodie admitted. "I was alone and frightened. Gerald found me and took me in for the night. Later he took care of the trust and my allowances until I was old enough to handle my own finances. I lost part of the memories of my childhood. It's a pretty common side effect of a major traumatic experience."

"And you haven't shifted since?" Tails asked.

"Not once," Brodie answered, pursing his lips together to form a thin line. "And that isn't going to change anytime soon. So you can tell your boss to forget it. I won't be joining in any fight. I've completely subdued my other half. "

"I'll try," Tails offered, "if you try to get some sleep. I know this is a lot for you to take in, but it won't do either of us any good if we are both grumpy from being overtired." She paused. "If I could make one suggestion, it would be that you stop thinking of yourself as two parts instead of one whole. The secret to controlling the shift lies not in overpowering the animal side, but in allowing it to meld with our human side. The two need to work together to form one person."

Brodie nodded, getting to his feet. "I never thought of it that way. Thank you." He glanced at the empty bed. "Would you lie with me for a bit?" he asked. "We don't have to touch or anything. It's been a while since I've had someone around and it kind of feels good."

Tails nodded, taking the spot beside him on the bed. It had been a long time since she'd had anyone around too. She turned on her side, her arm extending around his waist.

Brodie didn't have a lot of previous experience with emotional contact, but then she didn't either. Maybe they were exactly what one another needed. He glanced down at her head nestled into his chest. A warmth surrounded his body and soul. His nostrils flared, relishing in the light floral scent of her hair. It called his name, begging for one more whiff. The primal nature of his other side screamed for satisfaction. He silenced it. The moment would have been ruined by anything more. It might not have meant forever, but those few minutes were what made life worth living. Neither one of them was ready to take the next step in fully understanding or catering to another person. One day, when they were, he had a feeling they'd do it together.

"Tails," he whispered, under his breath. "I think your boss might be planning to take things a little farther than just equality."

She didn't answer and he didn't push the topic any further. He closed his eyes, listening to their heartbeats intertwining.

"Could you sing to me?" The words came from Brodie's mouth before he knew what they were. It was a strange request.

Tails didn't flinch, instead, she began humming a melody. The sweet sound of her voice mingled with a familiar tune. It was the same one his mother had sung to him as a child. He closed his eyes, allowing sleep to take him. There would be no nightmares that evening. A simple childhood song chased them all away.

# Chapter Twelve

"What did you say to him?" Tails questioned, taking a seat across from her boss. "He didn't say a word after we left, other than to let me know quite clearly he had no intentions of ever shifting."

"So convince him," Zeus replied, staring off in the distance, the blank gaze of thought visible in his eyes. "We need him."

"Why?" Tails questioned. "Why do you need him so much more than any other shifter we have met? What does he have that makes the difference between win and lose?"

Zeus cocked his head slightly to one side, the corners of his lips twitching. "What makes you think I am going to spill all my plans to you?"

"I need to know if I am going to get the results you want," Tails said. "I have to understand what is required of him."

Zeus huffed a chuckle. "I told you before, he's special."

"Special," Tails repeated. "Like me?"

"Don't flatter yourself," Zeus barked. "You have your uses, but you are hardly special. No, my dear, I am talking about evolution. Brodie was one of the first to exhibit the signs."

"How long have you been watching him?" Tails asked.

"For quite some time," Zeus admitted, emptying the contents of his glass into his mouth. He swallowed it back in one large gulp. "But the story starts long before that. It's amazing really. A single cell started everything. It grew and adapted, species after species, until finally humans were born." His lips pressed together, puckering out slightly. "And they thought they were the be-all and end-all of existence. They still do." He let out a throaty chuckle.

"I don't understand," Tails admitted, tossing a coin in the air. "What does this have to do with Brodie?"

Zeus ignored her interruption. "They weren't, of course. Then we came a long. Shifters were meant to replace humans at the top of the food chain, not be bound by it. We were too soft... let them control us for too long. Evolution doesn't care about our petty squabbles. It goes on doing its own thing regardless. So you ask why Brodie is so important? It's because he is the first in the line of a new evolution of shifters. This young species has not only the ability you and I do to change forms; they have additional gifts that make them stronger, faster, invulnerable. Some might even be immortal."

"Brodie," Tails said, "the guy upstairs? If he has magical powers he sure knows how to hide them well."

"Yes," Zeus agreed. "There was an unfortunate hiccup in my plans. It happened when I was first forming the club and the revolution. Not everyone saw things as clearly back then." He stared at the melting ice in his glass, swishing it around in circles. "I didn't have the tact I do now, or the finances. I handled things poorly. Of course, it wasn't for naught. I learned a lot from my attempted dealings with his parents." He sighed, shrugging his shoulders. "Things happen for a reason."

"His parents," Tails mumbled. "Were you watching him as a child?"

"Of course I was," Zeus scoffed. "He had the potential to turn the tides. I had hoped to bring him here to study and learn. Instead, things went awry."

"It's hard to believe that anyone wouldn't want to learn from you," Tails lied; she took his glass, refilling its contents.

"Indeed," he muttered. "His parents wanted to try a more diplomatic route in dealing with the humans. I tried to convince them this was best thing for Brodie, but they ran."

"Wait!" Tails exclaimed. "They literally ran?" Her hands rubbed the back of his neck and shoulders.

"That feels delightful," Zeus moaned. "They were convinced I'd end up hurting their son. They went so far as to burn their own house down, so there would be no evidence or trail to follow."

"What happened?" Tails whispered in his ear, allowing her hot breath to continue caressing the lobe at the end of her words.

"They were too slow," Zeus replied, rolling his head forward. "We arrived just as they were making their escape."

"But you couldn't catch them?" Tails asked.

"What makes you think that?" Zeus snickered.

"You didn't bring Brodie here," she answered, continuing to massage stressed muscles. "If you caught them, he would have been your priority."

"He was," Zeus admitted. "I made a mistake." He pulled her hand forward and kissed the back of it. "I underestimated his parents' commitment to their child. It was the first snowfall of the year. The roads were slick and their car spun out of control. We went to offer aid, but they were stubborn, insisting it was a ploy to take their boy away."

"Was it?" Tails questioned.

"I suppose it was," Zeus admitted, chuckling. "It wasn't planned that way, though. An argument erupted that escalated rather quickly. One thing led to another and... Brodie's parents didn't survive the confrontation."

"You killed them?!" Tails exclaimed.

"You sound surprised," Zeus said, turning to face her. "You have known from the start that sometimes there are casualties beyond our control. This was one of those cases. Unfortunately, with their deaths looming overhead, taking the boy would have raised too many questions around town. At the time, I wasn't able to handle such an investigation. I had no choice but to leave Brodie at the side of the road. It looked like an accident resulted in accidental deaths. I called a man that had been acting as a liaison between myself and his parents to pick Brodie up and watch over him."

"The attorney," Tails suggested.

"You catch on quickly," Zeus snickered. "Brodie trusted Gerald and I kept an eye on them both. I wasn't going to recruit him for a while yet, but the new laws changed my plans."

"You said Brodie was the next step in our evolution," Tails said. "What does that mean? I haven't seen anything extraordinary. If anything, he's a bit timid."

"He hasn't learned how to control it," Zeus explained. "Once he learns in shifted form, the sky is the limit. He needs a teacher."

"Should I be afraid?" Tails asked. "What, exactly, is the great power he alone posses?"

"I never said he was alone," Zeus replied, chuckling. "Only that he was the first of his kind."

"There are others?!" Tails exclaimed. "Why haven't I heard of them before?"

"You didn't need to," Zeus said. "And you still don't." He gulped back a mouthful of whisky. "This part doesn't concern you."

"It does if you want Brodie to shift," Tails argued.

"What do you mean?" Zeus questioned.

"The night his parents died, he fully shifted for the first time," Tails answered.

Zeus sat forward. "Remarkable. That's even further advanced than I thought him to be. What else? Tell me." He grabbed her wrist, squeezing tight. His blackened eyes bulged.

"He believes his shift was responsible for his parents' deaths," she squeaked, staring into the face of a madman. "He won't use his abilities because of that. That's all I know. You can let go now." She pulled back.

"Of course," Zeus said, releasing his grip. His voice softened. "He is quite fond of you, isn't he?" He tapped a finger on the arm of his chair. "I want you to convince him he needs to learn how to control his other side."

"If you want me to do that," Tails said, taking a step back. "I'll need full disclosure on what I am getting into. There's no way I am going in blind and getting myself killed. I want to see these others and what they can do."

"Very well," Zeus agreed. "We'll leave for the facility first thing in the morning. I'm placing my faith in your hands. I expect you to deliver results." He drained the rest of his second drink. A coin clanged against the glass, landing in the bottom, tails side up.

"I always do," she snickered, ignoring the rest of his words. "I'll be ready at the crack of dawn."

A low growl escaped Zeus's jaws, not knowing whether it wanted to be a laugh or a warning. "Oh and, Tails," he called out, "I hope you aren't thinking about developing feelings for this fella. I can't let anyone interfere with the plans, not even you. We are too close to the end now."

"You know all that matters to me is the cause," Tails stated, her face emotionless. "My only goal is to bring our kind the equality we deserve. That's what my mother would have wanted. She sacrificed herself for me. The least I can do to repay that debt is to honour my duty and help others avoid what she went through."

"That's my girl," Zeus snickered.

# Chapter Thirteen

"Was the blindfold really necessary?" Tails whined. The lack of sight made every bump in the road feel a thousand times harder. Her head bobbed up and down, neck straining to remain straight.

"There aren't many who know or remember exactly where this facility is located," Zeus answered. "I'd like to keep it that way. It isn't much farther. Once the main road is out of sight, I'll give you back your vision."

Tails blew a mouthful of air upward, blasting loose strands of hair off her face. It was a useless exercise. The wind sent them right back again. She'd wondered why they were taking an all terrain vehicle and not her boss's usual limousine. Now she had her answer. They weren't only heading out of town; they were going off-road. That explained the jerkiness of the ride as well.

Zeus knew shifters inside and out. He covered all the bases with a single vehicle choice, taking away the use of keen senses. The blindfold took care of her sight. Removing the top from the ATV created gusts of air that almost eliminated scents and background noise altogether. There was little chance she'd be able to retrace their journey at a later date, even if she wanted to.

The rev of the engine eased, the strong breeze slowing to an eerie draft. The skies had been sunny when they left the club, but the faint scent of moisture in the air warned of grey clouds moving in. A shock raced through her fingers from contact with the dashboard. The undeniable electrical charge growing around her could only mean one thing; thunder and lightning were imminent.

"How close is the storm?" Tails questioned.

"Too close," Zeus admitted. He ripped the blindfold from her face. "I was going to wait until we were inside, but we may have to make a run for it."

Tails gasped, watching the first of three gates sliding open. Terror from her past met the monsters of her present. She'd been there before. Her eyes fell on a decrepit sign swinging back and forth by one bolt. This place was the bane of her existence. It was her personal hell.

"This," she muttered, her mouth left hanging open without purpose. She'd never told him about her family's time there and the government had destroyed all records long ago. No one, including her boss, could have known that building was where she was conceived and born.

Zeus followed her line of sight. "You know your conspiracy theories," he said. "This institution was once used by humans to enact the most heinous of acts against our kind. I am impressed you recognized it. Very few have ever seen pictures. There were only a couple I know of who survived the government cover-up a decade ago. Keeping things under wraps is how the humans got away with it. The only headlines were in tabloids and labelled a hoax. "

"But why are we here?" Tails asked.

"I bought it," Zeus announced. His foot hit the accelerator as the third and final gate opened. The ATV jerked forward in a race against the impending weather.

"Why would you do such a thing?!" Tails cried out. Her heart rate quickened the closer they came to the building. There might have been a bit of extra wear and tear on the exterior, but other than that it was exactly as she remembered.

"Because it was the perfect solution to my needs," Zeus explained. "After it was shut down, the government wanted to bury the events that took place here. I can't blame them. The experiments they conducted were quite extreme. Even shifter haters would have been appalled by the brutality that went on within these walls. Reports came out, but were squashed before reaching mainstream media. Thus the exact location remained a secret, and they kept it that way. It was better than living in constant fear of the building being used for an uprising. Years later, it went on the black market at an extremely reduced price."

"You bought it because it was cheap?!" Tails squealed.

"And because even if someone were to know exactly where to come to find it, they wouldn't want to," Zeus answered. "Even the property surrounding the facilities is thought to be haunted by demons born from the purest of evils. I was banking on its reputation to mask my activities. It was a business decision, not an emotional one."

"With its history, I would have thought there would be those who would want to expose the truth," Tails argued. "Someone must want to find out what exactly happened here. The articles that were written are filled with speculation rather than truths. Reporters love a juicy story."

"Indeed," Zeus said, the ATV rolling to a stop by a side entrance. "The truth will never come out. I think most people realize that. There are no survivors from Area Fifty-Nine to tell their stories. There are no witnesses to collaborate with. There is no evidence to support theorist claims."

"There must have been some clues left," Tails suggested. "They couldn't hide all of it." The first raindrop hit her forehead.

"There were," Zeus said. "I'll explain more inside. Before we go in take a big whiff of the air. Smell beyond the rain."

Tails inhaled deeply, searching for answers. Her throat began to close, offended by the putrid scent of death. She coughed, wheezing for the oxygen her own body refused her. Zeus's hand grabbed her arm, pulling her into the building. Tails fell to her knees on the concrete floor.

"You see," Zeus said. "No one wants to know what causes pure evil to linger in the air. It's too vile for even the worst of humanity."

"Do you know?" Tails questioned, regaining her breath and stance.

"The grounds inside the gates are nothing more than a mass grave," Zeus explained. "Hundreds, if not thousands, of shifters who were tortured and murdered at the hands of humans are buried here. Most never even had a name. There are no birth certificates. No one outside these walls ever saw them. Their remains are the only proof they existed, and no one is coming to dig them up."

Tails glanced around, emotions overwhelming her reason. Tears stung their way into the corners of her eyes, threatening to fall. A subdued memory was attached to each one, surfacing for the first time in years.

"Relax," Zeus snapped. "This is only the entrance, much like the outside of the building is merely a ploy to throw off anyone who did make it this far. Farther in is where we are heading. I've had the interior completely remodelled."

A key turned three times before a buzzer sounded. He held the door open, motioning for her to enter. Every muscle in her body tried to refuse. If her boss had figured out her true nature, she was heading into a trap. On the other hand, if he didn't suspect her and she refused to enter, he'd know something was up. Her tongue darted out, wetting her lips.

"Is something wrong?" Zeus questioned, his brow forming an unusually high arch. His nonchalant expression turned sour.

"No," Tails lied. "The scent of death made me a little queasy. I'll be fine." She took the lead, holding her breath.

"Head straight through the next set of doors. They will open automatically as you approach," Zeus instructed. "We'll have to be decontaminated at that point. All of the areas beyond that are considered clean rooms. You don't mind sharing a shower, do you?" The sly grin of a demon crept over his face.

Tails swallowed back the lump forming in her throat. The thought of undressing in front anyone in such a disgusting place turned her stomach into knots. The feeling intensified, knowing her boss planned to scrutinize every inch of her naked body in the process. If this was a trap, he wanted to catch her using her abilities. Her body tensed at her inability to choose between modesty and survival.

# Chapter Fourteen

Decontamination was a nasty business that left her entire body aching. Reddened skin stung from having been blasted from all sides by streams of relentless liquid. At first she thought it was water, but once a drop found its way inside her closed eyes she knew differently. A powerful antiseptic had been mixed in; strong enough to leave exposed sensitive areas raw. The saving grace in it all; her boss didn't come near her through it all. He might have seen her naked, but that was as far as it went without using an ounce of her special abilities to keep it that way.

Glass doors slid open, offering temporary freedom. Tails scurried toward a pile of clothes awaiting her arrival. Hospital scrubs weren't her first choice in fashion, but it was better than walking around au naturel. Plastic slippers covered her feet.

"The head cap too," Zeus ordered. "We don't want any outside irritants to bother the guests here while they study their craft."

After the last of her long hair was tucked neatly away in the plastic cap, another buzzer sounded. A set of double doors swung open, revealing a pure white hallway.

Tails blinked, her eyes adjusting to the brightness. It was a completely different scene from the one that once existed. Back then, there was nothing but grey—it wasn't only visually, either—it was the atmosphere as well. Colours were thought to lend hope to prisoners, something none of them ever had. There was no mercy; no chance for rescue; and, for most, no escape. She had been one of the only survivors, although she didn't consider herself lucky. The horrors of her time there haunted her more than she admitted. It didn't matter how far inside she buried them, they still existed and always would— waiting for the opportune moment to arise from the depths to torment her again—moments like the one she was currently in.

"This is the main wing," Zeus said. He'd been chattering for sometime about the safety features he'd installed to benefit those training there. "Here take a look." He pointed toward a window that didn't face outside.

Tails peeked her head around the corner, looking into a plain white room. A boy tossed a ball against the wall, ignoring her altogether. "Can he see me?"

"No," Zeus answered. "It is better that way."

"He's just a boy," Tails muttered. Memories of her own childhood begged for caution in her wording. Her secret was one her boss could never know, especially not now. Her ties to the facility were a danger to him; one she doubted he would continue to allow to exist.

"That is how all prodigies start out," Zeus replied. "Do you have a problem with that?"

"No," Tails lied. "I guess I figured since Brodie was on the list, they would all be closer to his age. This one can't be older than twelve."

"Thirteen actually," Zeus admitted. "I only said Brodie was the first. After I lost him, I search for others. It was a number of years before any turned up. This one is the oldest of the group."

"Does he have a name?" Tails asked.

Zeus checked a chart on the wall. "Number 04398," he announced. "His ability includes the use of fire. I find elementals are the most interesting of the lot."

"But does he have a real name?" Tails asked.

"No," Zeus admitted. "We keep outside influences to a minimum. It's best for them that way. Emotional attachments tend to get in the way of their abilities."

"What about their parents?" Tails asked. "Or other family members? They must want to visit."

"Not at all," Zeus replied. "The majority of them were incapable of handling their child's unusual talents. It was quite a burden. Receiving money for me to take their problems away was a blessing. I haven't had a single issue... other than Brodie." He pressed a big green button on the wall.

The boy dropped to his knees, covering his ears. Pain inched its way over his face. He glanced up, letting out a noiseless scream that resonated in her bones. Fire filled their view.

"Impressive, isn't he?" Zeus asked, pressing a red button. The flames withdrew, leaving a view of the boy's body curled up in a fetal position on the floor.

"What did you do to him?!" Tails cried.

"It was a simple exercise to get him used to using his abilities," Zeus explained. "It is only a temporary pain... like a pin prick."

Zeus was the only prick in the room. He was torturing children to make them into his own personal army. "How many of them are there?" Tails asked, moving to the next window. A young girl sat cross-legged staring back at her.

"Twelve total," Zeus paused before adding, "worth working with."

The young girl's lips curled up into a snarl.

"Are you sure she can't see us?" Tails questioned.

Zeus chuckled. "Not in a conventional way. This one has a mind power we don't fully understand. She could be the strongest of the bunch once she reaches puberty. Right now she is limited to strong feelings. If you watch, her eyes will follow you as you move about. She knows someone is there, but doesn't understand why she can't visualize them. That frustrates her and usually ends in objects being tossed around in a tantrum of sorts. We had to remove all the furniture for her sake and the staff's.

"Don't you worry about your workers spilling the beans about this place?" Tails asked. "It must be hard to control them all."

"Everyone who works here is dedicated to the cause," Zeus replied, adding a laugh onto the ends of his words. "If they ever decide not to be, they will simply cease to exist. Before coming to work here, they were all outfitted with a tracker of sorts. If they try to leave the perimeter of the fence, the implant explodes, taking them with it."

"They are prisoners?" Tails asked.

"They volunteered, knowing the cost," Zeus explained. "Humans have dictated how shifters live for far too long. We finally have a weapon strong enough to defeat them. A weapon that, I might add, is almost ready to deploy."

"That's what you need Brodie for," Tails muttered.

"Smart girl," Zeus replied. "You felt his draw, I assume. He could command this group with a snap of his fingers. I need him here to lead and I need you to convince him this is his calling."

As if on cue, the sound of snapping fingers interrupted their conversation. A hairline crack in the window barrier grew in a similar pattern to ice crystals on glass.

"She's grown stronger," Zeus said, a wicked smile overtaking his face. "Don't worry. The containment will hold."

A green fogged poured in through a vent in the wall, forming a gaseous waterfall to the ground. It hung heavy, hugging the floor, slowly building in height. The girl held head her chin high, awaiting the unavoidable. It was only a matter of minutes before the effects took a hold of her. First came the suffocating cough, then her body went limp, and finally darkness took over. As fast as the substance had swooped in and wrapped around her, it disappeared again.

"She'll sleep for a few hours," Zeus said. "It will give workers a chance to reinforce her cell, adding another inch of thickness."

Tails opened her mouth, a complaint waiting to be unleashed. Before she could make a single sound, a scream interrupted her, ripping at her psyche with the power of a sharp blade cutting flesh. It wasn't a normal cry for help. This was the voice of the tortured. A noise that brought back the worst of her memories, making her blood turn cold. Her body froze at the sight of two men dragging a child, wearing only a white gown, down the hallway.

"What are they doing?!" Tails exclaimed.

Zeus's nostrils flared, taking in enough air to fill his lungs. "That subject was found incompatible with our needs, but is to be of use in another way."

"How?" It was the only word that would form. Her heart ached, anticipating the answer. A part of her already knew: this facility functioned no differently from the one it used to be.

"We need to know the extent of the diversities between us and them," Zeus said. "How they deal with the cold, the heat... if they are immune to certain poisons or diseases. It may seem cruel, but they are serving a deeper purpose in the end. Their lives will spare thousands in the war."

Tails tried to utter a few words, but her dry mouth refused. Once it fell open, it had no plans on shutting again for a while.

"I'm going to go have a chat with the workers," Zeus said. "Wait here."

He could have ordered her to fly to the moon and it wouldn't have mattered. His words never reached her ears. She fell to her knees, lost in the terror of her own memories.

*****

"Wait," her mother screamed. "Please don't take my baby. I'll go instead. Do what you want to me. Please."

Her begging earned her a swift kick in the ribs. "Get back," the guard snarled, his face shadowed by the hood of his cloak. They always hid themselves from the subjects. It was easier to be cruel when no one knew their identities.

A second guard grabbed Toni's arm and yanked her forward. She screamed, kicking her legs in an attempt to squirm loose. Self-preservation instincts made no sense. There was nowhere to run to. All that would come from her protests was a slower and more painful death.

Claude stood, holding his head high. "I'll go," he offered, his thin frame shaking from his own foolishness.

Tears flowed from their mother's eyes. She would lose another child that evening and there was nothing she could do to stop it. She crawled forward, kissing her son on the forehead.

Tails peeked out from her hiding spot under the bed. Her long silver hair fell over her face, hiding her trembling lips. She was the runt of the litter and useless for the tests. The doctors had said so. That was the only reason she hadn't been taken and was still alive. When the guards came, however, she still hid, frightened of what was to come.

The guard kicked her mother away again. "If you are in such a hurry to join your siblings, we'll take you both."

The screams that came next, ripped at Tails' heartstrings. They drowned out her mother's pleas and later sobs. All experiments were conducted down the hall, only a few rooms away. That night the building heard the howls that were reserved for summoning death itself. Her brother and sister called forth the Grim Reaper to take them from the misery this world offered.

Her mother stood, fingers tracing a ray of light around the door. It hadn't been fully closed and locked. Hands pulled Tails from her hideout, swooping her up into a mother's embrace. Tails watched the hallway growing smaller. The wails of her family faded the farther they ran. The guards had made a fatal mistake in taking two subjects to torture. It made then careless and sloppy.

Tails blinked a tear away, acknowledging her siblings' sacrifice, before being put down on the ground outside. Storm clouds swirled overhead, rain pelting against her skin in a torrential downpour. Thunder rumbled as a fork of lightning hit the generator. The gates malfunctioned, opening.

"Run," her mother screamed. "Don't look back and no matter what happens don't trust anyone. Never let them know about where you come from or your other side."

****

"Are you okay?" a woman asked, helping Tails to her feet.

"Sorry," Tails muttered. "That noise hit a cringe button." She forced a smile over her lips. "It took me by surprise."

"That's why we keep them in sound proof rooms usually," the worker explained. "Listening to them complain and cry all the time could drive anyone mad."

"Ah," Zeus said, returning. "Sorry about that. They aren't supposed to move the subjects around while there are visitors in the facility. It won't happen again, you have my word."

"The child?" Tails questioned.

"Will be thoroughly punished for its behaviour," Zeus replied. "That one won't last much longer anyway."

She'd seen enough. Brodie was right. Zeus didn't want or care about equality. He was hell-bent on world domination and at any cost. The tension between humans and shifters was merely a means to an end. He barked about the injustices that happened at the hands of humans, but was doing the exact same thing to the next generation of shifters. Simply brightening the colour of the walls and making the facility sterile didn't mean using the same tactics and experiments as her captors had become okay.

"Now that you know," Zeus said. "I trust you will help open Brodie's eyes. It is important he fully understand the situation."

"Of course," Tails agreed. "I plan on making sure he understands every detail. Give me a weekend alone with him, and I'll make sure you get a big surprise."

# Chapter Fifteen

Tails muffled a scream, hiding what was left of the noise in the sound of a slamming door. Her room was a little more comfortable than the other shifters had, but her jobs were also more extensive. In her line of business, bonuses were a part and parcel of jobs well done. Still, possessions weren't something any of them kept. Everyone who was part of the club led a throw away life. Memorabilia from the past didn't exist, the present wasn't worth making memories, and for the first time, she realized there wasn't a foreseeable future. The people who worked for Zeus were as expendable as his clothing—changed daily.

Her fists came down hard on a dresser. The mirror hanging on the wall behind it teetered from side to side, threatening to fall. She glared at the image staring back, a complete stranger. The idealistic girl who wanted to change the world to be a better place was gone.

The woman standing in front of her was undeniably beautiful on the outside. Of course, all shifters were. Tails hadn't seen it before, or perhaps she had and didn't pay any attention, but Zeus had one thing right; evolution was doing its job. Shifters were built better than humans. They were stronger, faster, smarter, and more desirable. This new species, her boss took credit for discovering, had their predecessors beat hands down. Zeus had been so caught up in his game of topping the food chain; he never noticed she was one of the next generation.

For all of her life, she'd thought she was the only one—a freak of nature—hiding in the shadows, hoping no one found out what she was capable of. There weren't a lot of pieces of advice she remembered from her mother. The one she did, however, had been to always keep her gifts a secret. She huffed, a chuckle tagging onto the end of her breath. It was clear now. Trusting no one was what had kept her alive and intact. Who knew what Zeus would have done to her as a child if he had discovered the extent of the powers she possessed?

Her fist made contact with the mirror, splintering it into a web of separate shards. There was no need to worry about seven years of bad luck when she was already serving a life sentence without any chance of parole. The part remaining in the frame showed a new picture, a woman who was much older. She was no longer seeing herself as she currently was. This was a glimpse into the future, a prediction of her own destiny if she continued on the same path.

The web-like cracks in the glossy reflection acted as wrinkles carved deep into her skin. That wasn't the only change to her appearance, though. The damage her punch had inflicted had left sections of mirror overlapping; causing her hair to appear matted and frayed at the ends. Shaking fingers reached up to caress what appeared to be dry cracked lips.

The aged woman she exchanged glances with had given up her will to fight, to care, to hope, to live. For the moment, it was an illusion, but it easily could have come to pass. They had one trait in common; they were both alone.

She stumbled backward, falling onto her bed. Her mother wanted her to be strong and rely on only herself. A lifetime of not trusting anyone had left with no other options. There was no one to turn to in her hour of need. There was no one to bounce her thoughts off of or to put her mind at ease that she hadn't done anything wrong.

She rubbed her eyes, trying to think of a way to set things right. It was an impossible task to carry out without help. Everything she knew and had been fighting for was a lie. There was never any plan for equality. She had been supporting one man's insane plan to take over the world. Everything Zeus needed had already been laid out at his fingertips. He'd used her grief as a war tactic, to convince her to do his bidding.

She had recruited most of the shifters herself. If she tried to tell them the truth now, Zeus would simply call her a disgruntled lover. He'd played his cards carefully, hiding all the aces up his sleeves. At this point in the game, all her chances of winning rested on others catching him cheating.

There was one other possibility: Brodie. If he agreed to help her, there was a slim chance together they could overcome the odds. Unfortunately, he was also the only one around harbouring worse trust issues than her own; not to mention they were an unlikely team. But if Brodie actually had the power Zeus thought he did, it could work.

Her lips pursed together, puffing out into a pout. She'd never admitted to liking anyone before, but Brodie had a way of making her see things differently. It had been him who opened her eyes to what was actually go on in the club. It was him who set her on a new path, one that led away from Zeus's control. At that moment, it was Brodie who made her think that maybe she didn't have to be alone all the time.

Her legs kicked against the bed, fists pounding on the mattress. She sighed. Emotions were too confusing. Life should have been easier.

Time was short and a decision needed to be made: go it alone and take her chances, or trust Brodie and take a chance on him.

# Chapter Sixteen

Brodie lay on the bed, the same as he did in his previous room, staring at the ceiling. The missing crack should have given him a little bit of relief, but it didn't. Instead, it made the whole situation that much more boring. He jumped at a soft knock.

"Come in," he yelled. It didn't matter who it was, at least it was a break from being cooped up. He was used to being alone, but imprisoned was a different story. Closed in spaces drove him to the brink of madness.

"Hey," Tails said, peeking in before entering. The door closed behind her. "I was wondering if you were up. I have some good news."

"Your boss is going to let me go?" Brodie asked.

"Almost," Tails replied. "He's letting me take you away for a few days, on a vacation of sorts." She licked the regret from her lips. More lies were only going to make explanations harder later on. Trust issues were bound to be a problem. There wasn't much she could do, though. It might have simply been a bad case of paranoia. After what she'd just witnessed, though, she was positive Zeus had microphones or cameras hidden about the premises somewhere. That was the only explanation for the amount of information he managed to gather on anyone and everyone. Sometimes it was eerie how the man knew things.

Tails always believed she was the one with the secrets. How naive that had been. Zeus had been the one in control from the beginning. She was a fly playing chicken with a spider, buzzing up and down, thinking her opponent could never win without wings. It was all fun and games until she fell into its trap. A second web had been constructed without warning. What was worse, the stupid fly always thought she'd be let go if ever the web were to snare her. A true predator never uses catch and release. With the second nature of a fox, she should have understood that.

"Where are we going?" Brodie asked.

"Grab a sweater," she ordered. "I'll tell you on the way."

He shrugged his shoulders. It wasn't as if he was going to get a better offer any time soon. Spending time with Tails was a much better prospect than a weekend alone with Zeus. The man was a dirty as a spoon lying on the floor in a greasy diner. The hairs on the back of his neck were willing to testify to that.

Silence grew between them, keeping them at arm's length from one other. It wasn't only the walk to the car, either. The drive was equally as uncomfortable. They might as well have been two teenagers on their first date. Brodie chuckled under his breath. Technically, that was the correct experience level to describe the entirety of his love life. He side-eyed Tails, wondering how much of Zeus's story had been true. It might not have been his business, but he couldn't help but wonder how many men had been in her life and how he stacked up in comparison.

"A motel?!" Brodie exclaimed.

"Stay here," Tails ordered. "I'll be right back." She disappeared inside the office, returning a few minutes later with a key.

She opened his door, bowing to him as he stepped out. "We are going to take a bus," she stated, leading him by the hand to the stop.

Their new mode of transportation arrived within moments. Tails took the lead, climbing the stairs first, and taking care of the payment for both of them. Choosing a seat near the middle, he glanced around at the solemn faces of weary travellers. The day had barely begun and their eyes already drooped, supported only by the bags underneath. They came and went, stop after stop. An hour passed before his companion made a move again.

"The next one is our stop," Tails said, rounding a silver pole with the ease of a dancer warming up in a strip club. She motioned with her head for him to join her by the steps, waiting for the doors to open.

Brodie swallowed the drool pooling in his mouth. Sometimes it was awkward being a guy. He stood, hoping no one would notice the bulge growing in his pants. The little move she had made with the pole was too much for him to handle.

"I'll wait for the bus to stop," Brodie insisted, sitting back down.

Tails motioned again for him to join her. "We need to move quickly," she said.

In his opinion, pineapple on pizza was the most disgusting thing in the world. He filled his mind with the image, hoping to ease his other desires. It wasn't an ideal plan, but at least it put a damper on things. He untucked his shirt, pulling it down over his jeans before fulfilling her request.

"The airport?!" Brodie exclaimed, taking all the stairs down in one leap. "Are we going on a trip somewhere?"

"Just follow," Tails replied, heading into one terminal and out another. She stopped at a sign for the airport parking lot shuttle.

Brodie eyed her with a quizzical brow, but figured there weren't any answers coming yet. Whatever they were doing, from the look on her face, it was important. He took a seat, preparing for the bumpy ride.

"Section A-three," Tails said to the driver. The man nodded, closing the doors.

There were a few other riders; each had a white piece of paper in their grips telling them where they left their car before heading off on vacation. For the most part, they kept their eyes a fixed on the ground and lips shut. One by one the shuttle emptied, until the driver called out their number.

"Follow me," Tails ordered, winding through aisles of cars waiting for their owners to claim them.

"Why did we get off at that stop, only to walk all the way over here?" Brodie questioned. Her odd ninja tactics were wearing thin on his nerves. Whatever game they were playing, he wanted to know the rules. "I think I've been as patient as can be expected. I'm not going a step farther until you tell me what's going on."

"This one," Tails said. "Get in." She glanced over her shoulder, then around the rest of the lot.

The taillights on a small green car blinked twice; the locks opening. Brodie took the passenger side seat, adding a few grunts to make his displeasure known. "All right," he snarled, "that's enough. I've followed you around for hours. I think I deserve an explanation."

"I had to make sure we weren't followed," Tails said.

"We could have watched out the back window of your car," Brodie argued. "That would have been a lot easier and less time consuming."

"I couldn't take a chance that there was a tracker on the car," Tails replied. "After what I've seen in the past twenty-four hours, I'm not sure if anywhere is safe." The engine of the car hummed with the turn of a key.

"Where are we going?" Brodie asked. "I think I deserve to know that much." He let out a huff, turning his head toward the passenger side window.

"I bought a piece of land with a cabin on it," Tail said. "No one else knows about it. We should be safe there."

"Safe from what?!" Brodie exclaimed. "Are you going to fill me in on the details?"

"Buckle up," Tails ordered. "I'll tell you as much as I can on the way."

# Chapter Seventeen

The dirt and gravel road wound in an S shape around trees of various types and sizes. Brodie watched nature passing by outside the window, as he listened to Tails explaining the horrors she experienced in the facility. He'd known from the beginning he hadn't liked Zeus. The scope of what the man was capable of he'd underestimated, though. Torturing children was beyond all reasonable thought. It didn't matter what the cause was he claimed to be fighting for. The rights of one were equal to the many in his books.

A log cabin came into view. Weeds grew as a welcome runner from the parking spot to the front porch, making it obvious that it had been a while since anyone had visited. Tails grabbed a key from a pot on a sill. The door creaked open.

Dust and stale air greeted his senses. Brodie snorted a laugh. It was a trick he'd learned long ago that made it easy to catch anyone masquerading as a friendly shifter. Allergies were a human shortcoming, making dust bunnies their true enemy. Sneezing gave them away every time. He hadn't had much use for that particular trap, but figured one day it would come in handy.

"It isn't much," Tails said, glancing out the back window at a small lake. "It could be a cozy place to live, though. There is enough land to grow some crops. It wouldn't be hard to stay off the grid."

"Are you asking me to stay here?" Brodie questioned, arching his brows.

"I guess I am," Tails replied. "I'm frightened. I don't know how I never saw the truth before. Zeus is obsessed and dangerous."

"I can't run away," Brodie said. "I don't think you can either. We need to save those kids and stop him. We need a plan."

"He's got an army at his fingertips," Tails mumbled. "He's been building this force for the last twenty years..."

Brodie grabbed her shoulders, forcing her to face him. "Is there something you haven't told me?" he asked, staring into her eyes.

"I only just found out," Tails stuttered.

"What?" Brodie asked, shaking her. His grip sank into her skin, leaving red marks.

"You didn't kill your parents," Tails whispered. "Zeus did. He wanted them to give you up. When they refused he lost control. Once they were dead, he couldn't take you. There would have been too many questions, possibly a full investigation. Instead he had your attorney watch over things. This new legislation that came out forced his hand before he was ready to play it. He needs you."

Brodie fell to the ground, his hands covering his face. "Why?" he asked. "What could he possibly want from me?"

"You are one of the next generation," Tails explained. "You were the first of your kind. He believes you have the ability to be the alpha of the entire species. If that's true, they would all follow you anywhere and do anything you asked. You could order them to fight, and with their power, wipe out entire cities in minutes."

"So he wants control of a puppet master in order to control the puppets," Brodie muttered. "Brilliant. I don't suppose you told him I won't shift. That might put a kink in his plans."

"I did," Tails said, kneeling beside him. "That's why he let me take you away. He tasked me with convincing you to help."

"And are you?" Brodie asked, his lips pursed tightly into one line. "Is that why you brought me here, to change my mind?"

"No," Tails blurted out, "and yes. I don't know what I was thinking." She fell into a sitting position on the floor.

"Why should I believe you?" Brodie asked. "How do I know this isn't one big set-up? You could be playing me right into your boss's hands."

"Because I am just as afraid of him as you are," Tails cried. "I'm a next generation shifter too. I've been hiding my abilities from Zeus since we first met."

"What abilities?" Brodie asked.

"It's hard to explain," Tails said, her thumbs twiddling. "I can make people believe things are happening. It is almost like an illusion, but stronger."

"The judge," Brodie mumbled.

Tails nodded her head. "I made him see what he wanted to see. It wasn't real."

"So Zeus and all the men he talked about," Brodie said. "None of that actually happened? You faked all of it?"

"Yeah," Tails admitted. "When Zeus started my training, he had me watch porn so I knew what men expected of me. It was rather disturbing, but I used the experience as reference to create the fantasy worlds they expected to see in exchange for whatever Zeus needed."

"Have you ever..."

"No," Tails interrupted. "I'm a virgin. I was so wrapped up in serving the cause, I never allowed myself to be close enough to anyone. I never wanted to before."

Brodie chuckled, earning him a swat in the arm. "Sorry," he said, his laughter tapering off. "Why are you telling me all this? You've kept your secret for such a long time."

"Because," Tails said, licking her lips, "I feel as if I can trust you." She paused, her heartbeat racing. "And I don't want to be alone anymore."

Their eyes met. He leaned in, his lips brushing against her. He watched her eyes close, preparing for a second kiss. He didn't keep her waiting. One hand cradled her neck, pulling her into a passionate embrace. Her mouth opened to his, their tongues intertwining in a moment of pure bliss.

"We'll figure this out," he whispered in her ear, nipping at it gently. "I promise we'll find a way. And when it is over, neither of us will have to be alone ever again."

# Chapter Eighteen

With contentment came the numbing effects of bliss. Brodie stretched out on the bed, listening to the sound of water. Steam escaped through the open bathroom door, a by-product of a hot shower. Moments later there was silence. Tails emerged, hair towel-dried and a kimono-style robe wrapped around her body.

"You planning on lying there all day?" Tails asked. "I thought we'd explore a few of the trails through the woods today."

"I was hoping you were coming back," Brodie smirked, patting the mattress beside him. "We could spend the day exploring in another way." His brows waggled in a humorously suggestive manner.

Tails chuckled, tossing a similar robe to her own on the bed. "Put this on," she instructed. "You are the one who gave me the confidence to stand up to Zeus and his army. That means we have work to do."

He groaned, rolling over to complain, but she was already out the door. Grumbling, he allowed the silky material to hug his frame. He shifted his shoulders, wishing the robe were a bit larger. The designers obviously had a much smaller physique in mind for their creation. The width of his frame alone made it a tight fit. He glanced down making sure everything was covered, before heading outside.

Tails was already at the tree line. Brodie snickered, his playful side set free. His heart pounded at the thought of a chase. This was his chance to take the advice Tails had given him. His two sides merged to form one. He was ready to allow them to work together in hunting down his prize.

The wind howled, indicating the game had begun. Lifting his snout in the air, he inhaled tracing only her sweet scent. A sly grin crept over his lips. He could pinpoint her location faster and more accurately than a GPS. His muscles tensed, pouncing into action. He'd already given her a more than ample head start, but it wouldn't last long. He was on the prowl.

A glimmer of her came into view, surrounded by an aura burning bright. Brodie came to a complete halt, enjoying the sight. Even from the back, she was the most beautiful creature in existence. Long silver hair swayed in the wind, its metallic qualities highlighted by a soft pink glow. Her kimono lowered, exposing the back of her shoulders. An exquisite fox appeared at her feet. It's rear shook, fur puffing. A display of magnificent tails fanned out. Only a peacock could have put on a better show. Woman and animal forms began as two then shifted into one. The robe fell into a pile. The human side vanished. The fox took a few steps forward. Extending her front paws, her head lowered toward the ground in a regal bow.

Brodie inched closer, taking a crouched position. One hand extended, gently caressing the fur on her head. "You are beautiful," he muttered. "And your name makes a lot more sense now." He chuckled.

The semi-circle of fluffy tails wagged their acceptance of his praise. Her head rose seconds before she leapt onto his chest, playfully nipping at his ears.

"That tickles," he complained, laughing.

She jumped back; retreating to the pile of silk she'd left behind. A moment later, Tails reverted to her human form, robe draped over her shoulders. "It's your turn," she said. "Show me who you are."

Brodie met her stare head on. "I - I," he stuttered.

"Your shifting wasn't what killed your parents," Tails said. "You have nothing to be afraid of. Give it a try."

Brodie nodded, a lump in his throat preventing words from forming. It was ironic how in stressful situations he could feel sweat forming on his brow and yet his lips managed to be completely dry. His tongue darted out, taking care of at least one of the issues.

Tails fell back on her heels from a kneeling position. Her eyes, filled with messages of support and warmth, never faltered from his through the entire shift. Her strength became his pillar.

Brodie gave in to his primal side, tossing his head back into a wild howl. Birds scattered from the trees, frightened by a ferocious predator's war cry. Two gigantic paws came down on the ground in front of him, sending out a mini tremor on impact.

It was Tails turn to inch forward. She extended one hand, head bowed, waiting for the massive beast before her to accept her as part of his pack. Zeus had been right. Brodie was the only Alpha male she or anyone else would ever need. He was magnificent.

Brodie sniffed her scent, instantly recognizing it. His rough pink tongue tasted her skin, first on the outstretched hand and then on her face.

Tails chuckled. "That tickles!" she exclaimed. "I guess it's payback." Her hand extending, running through his thick, white-as-newly-fallen-snow fur.

Brodie glanced deep into her eyes, seeing not her, but his own reflection. The red eyes that glared back shocked him into retaking his human form. Memories of his nightmares haunted him. His heart raced; sweat dripping off his brow.

"It's okay," Tails said, using her lap to cushion his head. "Everything is fine."

"No!" Brodie cried out. "It isn't fine. It is anything but fine. I know what my dreams mean now. If I ever taste blood, I won't be able to stop. It will change me. I don't want that to happen."

Her hand brushed through his hair. "Okay," Tails said. "We won't let that happen. We'll find a way to stop Zeus without killing anyone."

"Is that even possible?" Brodie questioned.

"We'll find away," Tails replied. "I can use some mind games, but only on one or two people at a time. If we are careful, we can still do this."

"What about after?" Brodie asked. "What happens to the kids... to us?"

"There is plenty of space here," Tails suggested. "We are off the main routes, so no one would find us, especially if no one was searching."

"Are you sure you want to settle down?" Brodie whispered. "That's a big step to take from what you are used to."

"I am," Tails replied. "Meeting you flipped my world upside down. You made me see things in a different light." She sniffled back happy tears. "I've never been more certain of anything in my life. I am in love with you. Apart, our confidence falters. Together, our resolve is strong. We can face anything side by side. I know it. My fears and apprehensions disappear when we touch."

Brodie bolted up into a sitting position. His hand gently caressed the side of her face. "I love you too," he whispered, leaning in. "Together is my favourite word."

Their lips met, tongues dancing a passionate tango. Brodie lay her on her back. With one arm on either side he hovered, keeping their bodies from touching. Her robe fell open.

Tails moaned. The heat of his breath tingled her sensitive skin with the lightness of a feather. She arched her back, begging for his touch. Ecstasy was his to give.

"We have a mission to complete," he whispered.

"Now?!" she exclaimed, panting.

"Oh, don't worry," he mused. "I won't let you go into battle all hot and bothered." A sly grin crossed his lips. The warmth of his breath left a trail on her body. Screams of pleasure awoke the woods, disturbing the birds from their nests for the second time that day.

# Chapter Nineteen

"Explain to me again why we are going back to Zeus," Brodie snapped. "It's like surrendering before we even try."

"I told you," Tails replied. "The only way we can get into the facility is if Zeus takes us there. He wants you to take an active role in leading his forces."

"You mean the kids," Brodie said.

Tails nodded. "As long as Zeus believes I am still on his side, he'll have no reason not to take us there. Once inside, we can do our thing."

"Our thing," Brodie repeated. "That's the part of the plan where we wing it and hope for the best, right?"

"Pretty much," Tails agreed.

"And how do we get out?" Brodie asked.

"I'm still working on that," Tails admitted. "There aren't any keys, all the doors and gates are operated remotely from somewhere inside the building."

"Great," Brodie said, rolling his eyes.

"Don't worry." Tails planted a kiss on his cheek. "It'll all work out somehow. The kids all have abilities too. Maybe one of them can help in the escape."

Brodie wiped the sweat from his brow and neck. "There is so much that can go wrong with this plan. The kids might not follow me. Zeus might have a trap set. The possibilities are endless."

"Don't go getting cold feet on me now," Tails said. "We are at the point of no return. Once we get out of the car, we have to go forward with the plan."

"I know," Brodie admitted. "I'm just a little nervous. I've never done any covert operations before, unlike some people."

"Shall we?" Tails asked, popping her door open.

"Here goes nothing." Brodie followed suit, walking directly on her heels in the underground garage. His hands extended in front of his chest, fingers locking together. A series of loud cracks echoed through the parking lot. "Sorry. I needed to loosen up."

Tails offered a sympathetic smile. "Oh," she said, pivoting. "Don't let him inject you with anything. That would be bad."

"Bad how?" Brodie asked, his brow furrowed.

"His workers at the facility were all implanted with bombs that explode if they try to leave the premises," she explained. "I don't think he did that with his test subjects, though. He needs them to be able to mobilize at a moment's notice."

"Wonderful," Brodie squeaked, his voice cracking. He cleared his throat. "Way to not stress me out before the main event."

Tails placed one finger over her lips. "Showtime," she mouthed. "Together."

The elevator dinged, doors opening to allow them passage in. Tails placed on hand on a scanner. Green lights flashed, confirming her identity. A second set of buttons appeared, each with its own letter in the middle instead of a number. She pressed on the C.

"C for club," Tails explained. "It isn't a difficult pattern to understand. It needed to be something that even the most basic shifted form could remember. Ease of operation but still too sly for human comprehension."

Brodie smiled, nodding at the tour-guide-esque information. She'd probably given the same speech a few hundred times to shifters being delivered to the mighty Zeus under the pretence he was working for their benefit.

The lift jerked to a stop, back doors opening to a room he was familiar with. Brodie glanced around, his gaze coming to rest on the man they had come to see. That was his cue. He took the lead, his stride strong and dominant. One hand reached out to offer in greeting. His strength poured into the grip as the two men connected.

"Glad to see you made it back," Zeus said, breaking the hold. "I trust you had a good time." He leaned into Tails, barely allowing his lips to brush over her cheek.

"We did," Tails answered, a coy smile plastered on her lips. It was better than cheap lipstick and just as effective. "I am happy to report, Brodie has made a decision... one I think you will be happy with."

"That is excellent news!" Zeus exclaimed, ringing a bell for service. "Champagne for my guests and myself," he ordered, clapping his hands together.

"I'm fine," Brodie replied, waving the waitstaff off.

"Don't be silly," Zeus argued, nodding to his employees to continue with his previous instructions. "We are celebrating a giant step toward equality for all of our people. One day this exact moment will be read in history books as the turning point in a revolution against oppression and injustice."

"I fear you put too much faith in me," Brodie said.

"Nonsense!" Zeus exclaimed. "I know it is true. Do you know how I know?" His lips quivered; excited about the secret they had to share.

"How?" Tails asked, accepting a thin flute off a silver tray.

There were only a few tried and true ways to tell the difference between a cheap glass and an expensive crystal one, other than weight. Learning to pick out knock-offs had been an unintended by-product of her training. Tails lifted her champagne in the motion of cheers, allowing light to pass through. The long stem drinkware she held was not only clear, but reflect a perfect rainbow prism. Her eyes twinkled, their natural beauty enhanced by the sparkles they were testing. Once again, Zeus had spared no expense in acquiring the best of the best for the patrons of his club.

"One of the subjects is a young prophet," Zeus replied. "She's seen what will come to pass, including you." He motioned to Brodie with his champagne flute. "I was skeptical, at first. That's when I decided to put her predictions to the test."

"What sort of a test?" Tails asked, pressing the glass to her lips—bubbles tickled them—but none passed through.

"It wasn't easy," Zeus admitted. "I had to work her day and night for a handful of visions I could use. It was worth it, though. That's how I knew about the classes Brodie was being forced to attend."

"That's how you've been getting all of your information," Tails muttered. She chuckled. "Here I thought you had the place bugged."

Zeus threw his head back into a howling laugh born in the deepest recesses of his throat. "And it didn't bother you?"

"Not at all," Tails lied. "Such a thing would only serve to upset those who have something to hide." Her lips puffed out, forming a pout. "Surely you don't consider me a traitor."

"Of course not," Zeus answered. "My subject told me you were dedicated to equality." He paused. "As she did Brodie as well. All of her bits of information have been spot on."

"What did she tell you about me?" Brodie questioned.

"That you were the one," Zeus admitted. "You would lead shifters to their destiny. Because of you, there would be peace between the races."

"That's a lot to throw on the shoulders of one person," Brodie said, rubbing his neck. "I'm not sure I see how I can be as important as you think I am."

"You are a born leader," Zeus explained. "Drink up and I will take you to my facility to prove it to you. Tails, I have some..."

"She comes with us," Brodie blurted out.

Zeus's head tilted slowly toward the man issuing him demands. "That's very bold of you," he mused. "You are barely a part of our organization. Barking orders at the leader isn't a wise move."

"I think I have some leverage," Brodie argued. "You need me. I don't need you. I am not asking a lot. I simply want Tails by my side."

"I warned you not to grow fond of her," Zeus said, pursing his lips into a barely visible line. "We all have our parts to play in this revolution, even Tails."

"Plans can be changed," Brodie rebutted. "Her role can be altered. Either you want me to join you or I walk. The choice is yours."

A sinister smile crept over Zeus's face. "Very well," he conceded. "I will allow it, for now. Don't think that means you will be issuing commands in other areas, though."

"He won't!" Tails exclaimed, coming between them.

Zeus pushed her aside. Their locked gazes threatened exploding fireworks.

"I have no desire to lead any revolution," Brodie snickered. "Like you said, we all have a role to play. Leader is yours. As long as Tails is by my side, I am at your disposal."

# Chapter Twenty

The blindfold hadn't bothered Tails the previous trip to Zeus's facility. This time, however, was a different story. Danger put its own spin on things. Knowing what her boss was capable of sent shivers down her spine and ice racing through her veins. Being without senses made things that much more unpredictable. Offering up the controls was part of the deal. The original invitation, after all, hadn't had her name printed on it. She was an afterthought... Brodie's afterthought. That wouldn't bode well with Zeus's ego. He wasn't a man to let anyone else call the shots, no matter how important they were.

"It seems longer," Tails yelled, receiving a mouthful of hair for her trouble.

"You are disoriented," Zeus suggested. "We are almost there." He pulled off her blindfold, exposing the approaching gates. "Brodie will have to wait until we are inside, though."

Brodie shifted his weight at the sound of his name. The trip was a practice run for his abilities. If faced with dark, he needed to be able to see. If sound was withheld, he needed to hear. If all of his senses were taken away, he needed to survive.

"Why?" Tails questioned.

"You underestimate the boy," Zeus replied.

"I'm right here," Brodie complained. "I'd prefer if you didn't talk about me as if I was in another room. It's annoying. Almost as annoying as being called boy."

Zeus laughed, masking the sound of the first set of gates scraping open. "Sorry about that, ole man," he jested. "I thought you fell asleep back there. It's your nap time, isn't it?"

"Not likely," Brodie snapped, his nostrils flaring. "Rain."

Tails glanced up at the grey skies. "It seems to rain all the time here," she said. "Is this the normal weather?"

Zeus glanced up. "I've never thought about it before, but now that you mention it, I suppose it does rain quite often."

"There's something else," Brodie said, sniffing.

"Ah, yes," Zeus answered. "The undeniable stench of death that resides on these lands. That definitely never goes away."

"No," Brodie said. "Not that. It's a sickly sweet smell carried on the winds. I've never experienced anything like it before."

"That's worrisome," Zeus blurted out. "There has been some talk about humans attempting to develop a new mind control drug. If they made it airborne, this could be a test run."

"What does it do?" Tails questioned.

"I can't be sure," Zeus replied. "Rumours are just that. If I were to hazard a guess, it probably makes shifters complacent. They'd like to turn us all into slaves, or pets... or pets that are slaves. This could be the first wave of an attack."

"Then we should hurry," Brodie suggested. "There isn't a moment to waste."

"Right you are," Zeus agreed. "This way." He took Brodie's arm, leading him out of the ATV and toward the building. The blindfold fell to the ground just inside the main entrance. "Here we are! The next room is decontamination." His eyes shifted between his two guests. "Under the circumstances, I think we can skip over those protocols. The team will need to be fully weaponized quicker than I anticipated."

Tails let out her breath. Stripping in front of two men had weighed heavily on her mind, as did thoughts of Brodie's possible reaction to another man seeing her wearing only a smile, and even that was questionable under the circumstances. Luckily, she didn't have to find out if her beau was the jealous type just yet.

This way," Zeus said, motioning toward the double doors. His hand slapped a large green button on the wall.

"Was that there before?" Tails asked, her nose scrunching up. She remembered the doors opening, but not a button. There hadn't been any of those until they reached the children's rooms.

"It's a command override," Zeus explained. "This whole facility is run from a central location. I and I alone have the ability to change normal procedures from other places around the building."

"So only you could chose a fast exit if a problem should arise," Brodie blurted out. "The rest of us would be locked in here until you gave the okay."

Zeus chuckled. "What in the world would make you think of that?" A grin that would put the devil to shame crept over his lips. "Of course, you are correct... if that was what I chose to do. This is my world, after all. This way." He pointed down the white corridor.

Tails took the lead, letting the two men stare each other down. Neither one wanted her to leave their sights, for completely different reasons. She stood in front of the first window.

Zeus nodded at the boy through the safety window. "There is your first test," he said. "Go in and talk to him."

Brodie grabbed the edge of a wall panel that jutted out. It closed behind him, not even leaving a hint of the seam where it had opened.

"Shouldn't we have told him about the boy's abilities?!" Tails shrieked. "He's completely unprepared. What if he can't control the boy?"

"Then he'll be barbecued," Zeus mused. "Either he is the one or he is not. Under the circumstances, I don't have time to play nice to find out." He slammed his palm against a button. Both the boy and Brodie fell to their knees.

"He's in trouble!" Tails screamed, her hands pounding on the glass. "You have to let him out. The noise is hurting him too."

"I can't let him out now," Zeus said, prying her hands off the clear surface. He held her arms back. "We'd both be burnt to a crisp as well. There's still a chance he'll pull a rabbit out of the hat."

"He could be killed!" Tails exclaimed.

"Yes," Zeus agreed. "Then we'd know he isn't the one we are looking for. It is the easiest way to gather the information we need."

Flames exploded, engulfing both bodies before seeking out every inch of the room. Hues of orange and red danced, knocking on the glass partition in a plea for freedom. Even being held back, Tails felt the heat slapping her across the face for ever thinking she could best her boss.

"Well," Zeus said. "That's unfortunate. I truly believed Brodie would be able to control the boy. This leaves us in a pickle, doesn't it? I'll have to initiate double, maybe even triple time, working with the subjects." He released his hold.

Tails' jaw dropped open, but no words formed. This wasn't one of the possibilities they had run through before agreeing to the plan. Every scenario they played out involved Brodie being the dangerous one. All of the attention had been on avoiding Brodie dealing a murderous blow, not him being on the other end of one. Her eyes stung staring at the room, still ablaze. In the background, Zeus continued to mutter about his ruined plans, although none of his words registered. Her eyes watered, stinging with the pain her heart felt. She turned her head as the blaze began to dim, not wanting to see how little remained when it retreated fully.

"Imagine that!" Zeus exclaimed, letting out a hoarse chuckle.

Tails lips trembled, curiosity demanding a peek. A part of her warned that her boss could have been goading her into seeing something horrible. Zeus's sheer happiness was impossible to deny, though. Her head turned slightly, just enough for a quick glance. Her heart skipped a beat. Twiddling thumbs became palms back on the glass again.

"He's okay!" Tails exclaimed. "I don't understand. We saw the chamber fill with fire. How could anyone survive?"

"Indeed we did," Zeus agreed, rubbing his chin. "I expect Brodie made it through in much the same way the boy survives his own attacks. Perhaps the subject shielded him. See the way they are embracing? Of course, the easy way to find out would be to ask him."

"Open the door!" Tails demanded, staring at Brodie, his arms wrapped tightly around the sobbing young boy.

"Patience," Zeus replied, holding up a hand. "It seems to me they are bonding. This could be an important step in Brodie's leadership abilities. If he has their trust, he has their loyalty. Let him have some time with the subject."

"How long?" Tails asked.

"Are you anxious to see him again, my dear?" Zeus asked, cocking his head toward her. "Don't tell me you have fallen for him."

Tails chuckled. "I'm more concerned about whatever was released in the air. I have no plans to give my free will to anyone, especially not our enemies."

"Hm," Zeus groaned. "I hope that is all it is. Brodie has a part to play. For now I am happy to indulge him to get the ball rolling. When the time comes, however, he will learn his place is much higher on the totem pole than yours." He grabbed her arm, pulling her to face him. "Having you by his side would only serve to bring him down in status. Do you understand?"

Tails pulled back her arm, nodding. "I understand fully," she answered. "I have no intentions of letting me or anyone else jeopardize Brodie's mission."

"Good," Zeus snapped. "Keep it that way. While we are waiting for him, I'll show you your room for the night."

# Chapter Twenty-One

Tails tossed a coin in the air and caught it again on the way back down. Each time heads remained face down. That trick was an easy one. Figuring out how to get out of the situation she was in was a lot more difficult. She side-eyed the open door, waiting for the next shift change to pass by. They came like clockwork every three hours. Heavy footsteps were exactly the same number every time and led to the only area besides the subjects' rooms she wasn't allowed to explore.

Either Zeus completely trusted her or he was planting bait to establish where her loyalties lay. He'd given her free rein of most of the premises. Of course, the area she was interested in lay in an authorized personal only section. That had to be the way to the controls.

Tails had already poked her nose in most other spaces, finding a fully stocked kitchen, additional bedrooms, and the bathroom. She'd even made a quick visit to the subject rooms, finding Brodie visiting with a different child.

In essence, Zeus had managed to effectively isolated Brodie, making any part he had to play in their plans impractical. Odds were he didn't have any clue he'd done it, either. It left her in a pickle, though. She was going to have to go it alone. Any chance for an escape officially rested squarely on her shoulders. The weight was already bogging her down.

Her abilities were great, one-on-one. Taking on the entire population of the facility, however, wasn't going to be easy. A nail clicked between her teeth. She glanced at the mangled remains. Biting her nails was something she hadn't done since she was a child.

The sound of shoes on the hard floor caught her attention. The regular shift had already passed. If whoever was wandering about had access to the locked areas, it was possible to find a way in. There were a lot of ifs in her plan, but it was better than nothing. Zeus was too cunning not to have a plan on how to control Brodie. The longer they lingered under his firm hand, the harder it would be to escape him.

Tails jumped to her feet, poised to make contact with whoever was about to cross her path. She leaped out, banging head first into a firm chest. Her eyes glanced up, their silver colour developing a glowing pink background.

"Sorry," she whispered, biting her bottom lip.

"No problem," the man said, looking straight into her eyes. "Is there anything I can do for you?"

"I was hopping for a tour of the facilities," Tails suggested. "Perhaps ending in a private room somewhere..." Her voice trailed off.

A smile crept over the man's face. "We don't get visitors very often, especially not the beautiful sort. Do you have clearance?"

Tails glanced at the badge on the man's white jacket. A slender finger tilted his head toward her chest. His gaze fixated on the cleavage displayed by a low-cut dress, barely taking stock of the clearance badge attached to one side.

"Looks good," he said, swallowing hard.

Her hair flipped back, allowing him direct line of sight to her hourglass figure. "Good," she said, giggling flirtatiously. Sometimes men were too easy to trick. This one hadn't even noticed she changed clothes mid conversation. Her disgust remained hidden beneath layers of illusion.

"This way," the man said, offering his elbow for her to latch onto. "I'm Larry."

"You can call me Tails," she replied.

"That's an unusual name," he said, his breath shaky.

"After the tour, I'll show you where I got it," she promised. "I think you'll enjoy the story." In his vision, her eyelashes batted seductively, instead of her actual gesture—an eye-roll. It was always the same. Zeus had taught her well, and in the end, that would be his downfall.

Access to the forbidden area wasn't nearly as interesting as she had hoped. Behind closed quarters lay more white corridors that intersected with one another. Tails counted footsteps and doors, hoping something would jog her memory if she needed a quick escape. With the way things had been going, there was no telling if she'd be able to follow through on this latest plan or if Zeus would be waiting to thwart her every move.

"This room controls the air in the building," Larry said. "There are regulators that keep the temperature exactly the same. One tiny shift and the heating or cooling kicks on automatically to rectify. Would you like to see it a bit closer?" He waggled his eyebrows suggestively. "No one ever goes inside..."

She batted his shoulder, giggling. "A girl can't give in at the very first room," she teased. "Besides, it's the big controls that get me all riled up. Show me what you really do."

Larry smacked his lips. "All right," he agreed. "My shift is coming up," he checked his watch, "in fifteen minutes. I am not supposed to take anyone inside, though."

Tails watched a second version of herself playing with Larry's shirt buttons. Her finger trailed down to his belt, before pulling away. "That's too bad," she said, adding a full pout for good measure.

"I could stash you away in another room until shift change was completed," Larry offered. "Then come get you after." His tongue slathered his lips in drool. "If you promise not to say a word."

Tails' illusion held up one hand. "I promise," she said, giggling.

# Chapter Twenty-Two

Tails crossed her arms over her chest. Allowing herself to be left inside what amounted to a furnace room wasn't an example of her finest work. Larry was taking too long to return. Her abilities were more to change what people saw rather than actual mind control. For all she knew, he could have locked her in before going to fetch Zeus.

She huffed, her bangs blowing off her face. The equipment around her might have kept the rest of the facility at a reasonable temperature, but in that small space it was as toasty as a room with three blazing fireplaces. She peeled off her sweater, using it to wipe the sweat from the back of her neck. Thankfully, the dress was only part of her illusion. The actual outfit was in her closet and the material it was made from didn't do well when paired with sweat. The fabric would have been clinging to her skin and most likely a bit see-through. The door creaked open.

"Hey," Larry whispered. "It's safe to come out now."

Tails jumped to her feet. "Thank goodness," she snapped.

"Is everything all right?" Larry questioned.

Tails scrambled to recover. "Fine. I was worried we wouldn't have much time together to have some fun. That's all."

"Don't worry, we have plenty of time," he nodded, a sickening smile plastered over his face. "There won't be a soul in this area for at least an hour."

"Well then," Tails said, licking her lips, "why don't you show me everything you..." She giggled, covering her mouth with one hand. "I mean the facility has to offer a girl. I think it will be a most fulfilling tour for both of us."

Larry smiled. He grabbed her arm, pulling her down the corridor to a red door. "This is it," he said, adding a wink to the end of his sentence. "Inside is everything that controls the entire facility."

"Everything?" Tails repeated. "You can pour out poison in any room, or set off sprinklers?"

"Uh-huh," Larry replied. "And so much more."

"You must be very important," she said, her lips puffing out kissing the air. "I bet you could show me a thing or two in there."

"I sure can," Larry agreed, adjusting his pants. "I think we better get inside quickly. I need to show you my control knob."

Tails raised her upper lip in disgust, although her tour guide never saw it. To him she was a woman completely smitten by his male prowess. She turned inside the door, watching him eyeing the other version of herself with lust.

"What do these do?" Tails questioned, pointing to a few large buttons.

"Don't touch those," Larry ordered, taking her hand away. "Those are the kill switches."

"Those kill people in various rooms?!" she shrieked, one hand covering her heart. "Oh my, I could have been a murderess."

"No. Those are literally the off switches for the entire facility. They are an emergency shut down. They cut the power, open all the doors and gates." Larry chuckled, grinding up against the control panel.

Tails watched the man fondling the air. She giggled. It was always amusing to watch someone making out with nothing.

Larry dropped his pants to the ground. "Oh yeah. You feel so good, baby." In his perception her butt was planted firmly against the control panel; legs wrapped around him.

Tails reached around him, pressing all of the buttons. Larry froze when the lights went out. "Don't stop," she cried out. "Please, I'm so close."

"I have to fix the controls," Larry argued.

"Please," Tails begged. "Fix them after you fix me." She glanced back from the door, to make sure Larry was enthralled in passion. Satisfied he would be kept busy for at least a couple of minutes, she raced down the hallway.

Voices heading her way made her duck back into the furnace room. Shouting became louder as a repair team closed in. Zeus barked a few orders to get the system back on line immediately. As words faded, she snuck back out and bolted for the only exit.

"What in the blazes are you doing?" Zeus yelled in the background. "Someone clean up these controls. This is disgusting."

A gunshot sent shivers racing down her spine. There was a moment of remorse for Larry, but he'd signed up for a suicide mission. It wasn't as if he would ever leave the premises. The moment the facility served no further use, all of the employees there were dead. They just hadn't realized it yet. Zeus probably wouldn't have said a word, either. Once he and his subjects were clear of the area he'd activate the bombs inside each of them. That would take care of witnesses and any physical proof left behind. At least Larry went out on a high.

Confusion filled the halls. Tails pushed past employees, trying to make sense of the sudden darkness. Keeping one hand against a wall she made her way back to the test subject rooms, a place no one else wanted to be.

"Brodie!" Tails called out. "Brodie!"

"I'm here," he called back.

Tails headed toward his voice. Her nose rose, searching for his scent. One whiff and her muscles released their tension. "Thank goodness." She threw her arms around his neck.

"What's going on?" Brodie asked.

"We have to go now!" Tails exclaimed. "The power is cut and the gates are opened, but it won't take them long to get it all fixed." She grabbed his hand, pulling him toward the exit. "Tell them to follow you."

Outside an emergency light shone down on the pouring rain. Tails glanced at the ATV and then back at the group.

There was no way they could all fit. Her eyes searched the lot, coming to rest on a small truck.

"Over there!" Tails yelled. "You drive. I'll get them all in the back."

Brodie nodded, heading for the front cab. He slid a small window open to allow him to communicate with his precious cargo. "Hurry! Zeus is at the door."

"Go!" Tails yelled, slamming the back gate to the truck closed. "We're all in." She stumbled forward as the engine raced.

"We won't out run him!" Brodie exclaimed. "He's following."

"Keep driving," Tails said. "I need all of you to stay sitting down and hang onto each other. Okay?" She gripped a bar attached to the interior wall of the truck, making her way toward the back gate. Every bump threatened her footing. Still she swung the door open, gazing straight into the eyes of evil on a rampage.

"Be careful," Brodie called out. "There is a ridge up ahead. I can't promise there won't be any big bumps."

"I'm fine," Tails said, hanging on tightly. Her silver eyes swirled with hues of pink, releasing a power unlike any she had attempted before. This time, it wasn't an illusion of herself she was creating. An entirely new road appeared for Zeus to follow. She blinked twice, releasing her gift as the vehicle pursuing them slid two tires off the road. "Stop,"

Her feet hit the ground running before the truck fully stopped. The ATV teetered on the edge of an overhang.

"Help me," Zeus ordered, stuck inside.

Tails bit her lip. She glanced down at him and then over her shoulder. Brodie was an angel. If he reached them, he'd insist they save Zeus's life—and as a reward—he'd make them pay for it each and every day for the rest of their lives.

"What are you waiting for?" Zeus cried. "Get me out of here."

"I can't do that," she replied, bushy tails fanning out behind her.

"You did this," Zeus mumbled. "You are one of them. I never knew before. I'm sorry. Things can be different now. I promise."

Tails held up a coin. "Call it."

"You're kidding," Zeus complained.

"Call it!" Tails repeated. "I'm giving you a chance. Make the right call and I'll save you." She flipped the coin in the air. "Call it now!"

"Heads!" Zeus yelled.

Tails watched the coin fall, without making any effort to stop its tumble. It twisted and turned before landing on the dashboard.

Zeus glanced down, his eyes glazed over realizing this was one game he was destined to lose. The ATV creaked forward.

Tails chuckled. "I told you before, tails always wins."

"I found some rope," Brodie said, rushing to her side in time to see the wheels slip and the ATV go over the side. It rolled down the hill, exploding into flames at the bottom. "I'll go down."

Tails put her hand up to stop him. "It's over. We are all free. With Zeus gone, no one will come looking for us. They need you." She nodded at the faces peering out of the back of the truck. "I need you. Let it go."

Brodie glanced over the edge.

"He didn't make it," Tails said. "If it makes you feel better, call for an emergency rescue when we are safely out of the way. It'll raise questions, though. The workers at the facility can't leave the grounds. I'm pretty sure they'll all blow up if Zeus doesn't check in. I'd hate for more people to be caught in the crossfire."

"Where to?" Brodie asked.

"Home," Tails replied.

# Chapter Twenty-Three

"I hope there's something tasty to eat," Brodie said, heading to the sink to wash his hands. "I'm starved and the kids are, too."

"Dinner will be in ten minutes," Tails said, swatting his hand before he had a chance to pull the lid off one of the pots on the stove. "You can wait!" She shooed him away. "How's the gardening coming along?"

Brodie flashed a toothy grin. "The kids are loving playing in the dirt," he answered. "We should have some fresh produce in a couple of months." He turned up the volume on a small television hanging on a wall.

"This just in," the anchorman said, pressing on the receiver in his ear. "A group of freedom fighters has claimed responsibility for releasing the substance that has been dubbed the *Peace Drug*. In a statement, their leaders claim the air born particles shut down use of negative emotions for a short period of time. The attack was not carried out on any specific race, but targeted the general population. Government authorities are calling the group's activities terrorist in nature. Overwhelming support for both sides is being reported all around the globe."

Brodie muted the news. "I guess that's what I smelled back at the facility."

"It's probably the reason why we didn't have to go through decontamination," Tails replied, wrinkling up her nose at the thought. "That hurt."

"What I don't get is it seems everyone forgot about the humans versus shifters battle. I never thought I'd see the day." He took a seat at the table, chugging back a bottle of water. The plastic crinkled in his grip once emptied of its contents. He tossed it in a recycling bin.

"I'm not surprised," Tails said. "They have been united against a common enemy, whatever side they are on. It's the same as when you hurt a finger. If you stub your toe right after, the finger isn't a problem anymore."

"So everyone simply moves on?" Brodie questioned. "There have to be people who still despise those who are different."

"There are," Tails answered. "But for the moment, they are more worried about never being able to feel prejudice or hate again. No one knows what this *Peace Drug* could do if released in larger quantities. I'm just not sure blocking emotions is the safest way to go about things."

"It isn't the worst thing that could happen, either," Brodie argued.

"I know, but it messes with our freedom. We have a right to chose, even if we make poor choices," Tails said.

Brodie placed a finger over his lips. "Shh. We don't want the kids hearing that sort of talk." He chuckled, pulling her onto his lap. "They'll be coming in any time. How about a smooch before they show up?"

"Get a room!"

"George," Brodie said. "Since you are interrupting a beautiful moment, you can help set the table. Wash up first."

"Great," George complained. "Blame the kid 'cause you two are being all lovey-dovey at the dinner table." He tossed a cap onto a wooden peg on the first try.

"Not again," a girl complained, dirt smudged over her nose and cheeks. "I thought hormones calmed down when you got old."

"Hey," Tails complained. "We are not old! Call your brothers and sisters in to eat." She stood, heading to the cupboard. "Then go wash up." She reached up, using every inch of her height and tiptoes to reach the plates.

Brodie came up behind her, taking them down with ease. "I got this," he offered. "That's what a family is all about; everyone doing their part to work together."

Tails smiled. Brodie was born to lead. She and the children had become his pack, which translated into family in human terms. Their struggle wasn't completely over. She knew that at any time things could become dire once again. They each had a secret to carry as well. Their extra special abilities would make them a threat in the eyes of humans and shifters alike.

The property she had bought was the perfect hideout. They were almost completely self-sufficient there. The day would come, however, when the children would want to forge their own place in the world. Dread filled her heart at the thought. There was little anyone could do about it, though. She and Brodie would teach them as best they could. Anyone who was prepared had a better chance of survival.

"Hey," George called out. "We're hungry over here." He banged his fork and knife blunt side down on the table. "How about some grub?"

Tails laughed, placing a large pot of stew on the table. She took a few steps back, admiring her family. Worrying about the future had never done her any good in the past. It was time to enjoy the present. Life wasn't about to get any better than it was right then.

The End... or is it?

# BONUS CHAPTER

Secretary of Defence Petra Dillon paced the hallway, waiting for the last of those summoned to arrive. This meeting was crucial to the overall protection of the country, especially if new terrorist threats were connected to old ones. Her thoughts raced a mile a minute, mulling over the information she had to share.

"You'll wear the carpet thin if you keep that up, Madam Secretary."

"General Taggart!" Petra exclaimed. "It's about time you arrived. The others are already waiting. I trust you have had time to review the information we sent."

"It's good to see you too, and I have," he answered, taking her hand between his in a friend gesture. "I'm not sure I understand why we are so interested in a chunk of land the military sold off years ago, though. Some things are better left undisturbed, if you know what I mean. "

"Come inside and I'll explain everything I know." A swipe of her security badge opened the wooden door beside them. "After you. Please have a seat." She motioned toward the sole empty chair left at the table, besides her own.

Taggart eyed the group of high-ranking politicians and combat officers. "This is a rather impressive gathering of the minds for merely discussing a couple of hikers and an accident on privately owned lands. What's this really about?"

"I trust I don't need to rehash old stories about Area Fifty-Nine," Petra said, "or the reason why these particular lands were sold off when they were."

"I think you can spare us the history lesson," Taggart agreed. "I try to avoid bring up the horrors of the past before lunch."

"Our team of scientists have ascertained that the latest terrorist attack could have only originated from four different and strategically placed regions," Petra explained.

"And Area Fifty-Nine is one of them?" Taggart questioned. His brows arched, forming a letter M on his forehead. "Isn't that a shock!"

Petra shook her head, trying to avoid smiling at the comment. "It only stands to reason that our military first acquired the property for its location," she continued. "Too bad no one thought of that when they disposed of it. There is a high probability that the air born drug was released there. We've had eyes in the sky and ears on the ground since."

The President's personal liaison, Todd Monroe, cleared his throat. "And all you have managed to come up with is two trespassers and an accident victim? That doesn't seem very impressive."

"It might appear that way on the surface," Petra argued. "The circumstances are unusual, however."

"Explain," Monroe ordered.

Petra held back the urge to roll her eyes. She didn't care who Todd Monroe was representing. If he kept his mouth shut, he'd have the answers he was demanding. "The two hikers called in an accident they stumbled upon."

"Am I to understand we have people watching the area and the only reason we know about this incident is because the hikers called us?" Monroe interrupted. "That's even less impressive."

"It's a rather large area," Petra replied.

"Yes or no, Secretary?" Monroe ordered.

"Yes," Petra replied in a huff.

"Todd, if I may offer my input," Taggart said. "I think the skills our forces have in gathering information is probably the least of our concerns at the moment. Perhaps we can allow Madam Secretary the opportunity to explain exactly we were brought together on this fine day."

Petra offered a grateful glance in the general's direction. "Thank you," she said.

"Very well," Monroe added, tossing his pen on the table and slouching back. "We'll leave inadequacies to a later date. Continue telling us how a pair of hikers are a threat to national security."

"It isn't the hikers so much that brings the concern. Although, they aren't beyond suspicion as of yet. The area, after all, is an odd place to chose for a leisurely stroll," Petra advised.

"Then why are we here?" Monroe complained.

"It's what the pair found," Petra replied. "They stumbled upon an accident that took place some time ago. A vehicle fell from a dirt road, ending up at the bottom of the ravine."

"Did it survive?" Monroe scoffed, rolling his eyes.

"No," Petra snapped. "It was completely mangled and burnt. Although, why any one was driving about harsh territory in an unregistered off-road vehicle is curious. What was even more disturbing was the man they found, still alive."

"Who is he?" The general questioned.

"We don't know," Petra admitted. "He's in a coma. Dental records came up blank. He has no fingerprints or other identifiable marks. His face was badly injured in the crash. Not even facial reconstruction specialists can piece it back together."

"I assume he wasn't carrying any identification," Monroe said.

Petra chuckled. "No," she answered. "We did check that first. He wasn't carrying anything other than a coin. It doesn't appear to be anything out of the ordinary, though."

"Haven't you tested it?!" Monroe exclaimed.

"We would if we could pry it from his grip," Petra answered. "The man simply won't let go."

"Do you believe this man was one of the ones responsible for the Peace Drug?" Taggart questioned.

"It's a distinct possibility," Petra replied. "He was in the right place at the right time. Unfortunately, we can't question him as of yet. We have a team of doctors working round the clock. Hopefully they can help him recover."

"Bring back a man from the brink of death to execute him for his crimes," the general scoffed. "Some tactics never change."

"Why change what works?" Monroe replied. "The hikers... I trust they are still in our custody?"

"Of course," Petra answered.

"I want a full interrogation conducted," Monroe demanded. "Use whatever means necessary."

"Are you suggesting we torture the couple?" the general complained. "Is that really necessary for being Good Samaritans?"

"Those responsible for the Peace Drug have clearly stated they had no plans to hurt anyone," Monroe advised. "Bleeding heart types wouldn't be able to leave an injured man to die. If you ask me, the hikers are the more likely culprits in this scenario."

"Understood," Petra said.

"Keep my office apprised of any updates," Monroe added. "I want to know when the man wakes up and the second anyone squeals." The edge of his folder banged against the table, straightening the papers within. "If you are through, I have other pressing affairs to attend to."

Petra nodded. "Thank you for your time."

"No need for thanks," Monroe scoffed. "I didn't have a choice in the matter. There's an election year coming up, after all." He exited the room without another word. An entourage of officials followed like ducklings chasing after their mother.

Petra exchange glances with the only other person left in the room: the general. His eyes laughed, forming wrinkles in the corners, before a he snorted a hearty chuckle. "That man has far too many pencils up his butt."

"You shouldn't say such things," Petra replied, stifling her own laughter. "If he heard you, he could strip those bars off your uniform."

"Ah, I'm too old to worry about snarky young politicians like him." Taggart waved his hand in front of his face. "With what the world is coming to, early retirement doesn't sound so awful."

"We need you, General," Petra suggested. "I know I do. You keep me sane at these meetings. Besides, you are the closest thing we have to a specialist when it comes to Area Fifty-Nine."

"That's one title I'd prefer not to have," Taggart admitted. "Has anyone contacted the property owner yet?"

Petra sighed. "It's a numbered company owned by a long line of other number companies. It's going to take some time to sort out what's what. Whoever bought the place didn't want anyone to know."

"That makes sense, given the nature of what went on there," Taggart mumbled. "I can't think of many people who would want to be associated with the place."

"Did it really happen?" Petra questioned. "Was our government involved in those experiments?"

"Do you really want an answer to that?" The general side-eyed his friend. "I didn't think so." Placing his hat on his head, he clicked his heels together. "I bid you good day, Madam Secretary. I'll begin my own investigations as well."

"I trust you'll keep me in the loop," Petra called after him.

General Taggart merely waved his hand above his head and kept walking. There were some things he never intended to disclose.

# *Author's Message*

I hope you enjoyed reading Tails Always Wins as much as I did writing it.

If you'd like to hear more about Tails and Brodie, please leave a review to let me know.

Until next time... happy reading!

# ABOUT THE AUTHOR

C.A. King is the recipient of several awards, including: The Hamilton Spectator Readers' Choice Award for 2017 & 2018 Best Author; The Brant News Readers' Choice Award for 2017 Best Author; Readers' Favorite award in the short story/novella category; the 2017 SIBA Award for Best New Adult; the 2017 SIBA Award for Best Novella; 2018 Readers' Favorite International Book Awards: Gold Medal in the Fiction - Supernatural genre; and 2018 Readers' Favorite International Book Awards: Bronze Medal in the Fiction - New Adult genre

Currently residing in Brantford, Ontario Canada, she lives with her two sons. She began her writing career after the tragic loss of her parents and husband. Redirecting her emotions through writing became therapeutic in her battle with depression and in 2014 she decided to publish some of her works.

# Other Titles from C.A. King

## The Portal Prophecies

These great titles in C.A. King's The Portal Prophecies series are available now at most online book retailers:

*A Keeper's Destiny*

*A Halloween's Curse*

*Frost Bitten*

*Sleeping Sands*

*Deadly Perceptions*

*Finding Balance*

*Volume I (Books 1-3)*

*Volume II (Books 4-6)*

The prophecies are the key to their survival. Can they solve them in time?

---

## Shattering the Effects of Time

Join the Shinning brothers, Jessie, Dezi and Pete as they set out on a quest to save their younger sister. No magic known to them or their friends has ever been able to reverse the grip of time. A few legends, however, exist mentioning ancient items that may hold the key to do exactly that.

This brand new series will take you on a search for the Fountain of Youth and Mermaids; a quest for the Holy Grail; a trip to visit Daryl the mountain guru, in the hunt for the Cinamani Stone; on a search for Ambrosia, the food of the Gods; and other adventures.

*Surviving the Sins:*

The prophecies are being rewritten. This time someone is using the seven deadly sins: Lust; Gluttony; Greed; Sloth; Wrath; Envy; and Pride, to unlock an ancient evil. The book falls into Jade's hands to answer destiny's call. Can she survive the sins?

*Book 1: Answering the Call*

*Book 2: Pride*

*Book 3: Lust*

*Book 4: Gluttony*

*Book 5: Wrath*

*Book 6: Envy*

*Book 7: Sloth*

*Book 8: Greed*

## When Leaves Fall: A Different Point of View Story

Ralph wakes up to what others only experience in a nightmare. Chained to a shed, he has no idea where he is, or who his captor is. His memories a blurred at best. As the days press on he finds himself experiencing a roller coaster of feelings. Hunger, thirst and pain become his only companions. Flashbacks of a happier time are all he has to keep him going. As his situation deteriorates, he finds himself doubting the very things he wants most -- a family.

*When Leaves Fall* is a dramatic-thriller with a twist. Keep the tissue box close for the ending.

## Tomoiya's Story

A Vampire Tale. She had a secret but she wasn't the only one who had something to hide.

Book I ~ Escape to Darkness

Book II ~ Collecting Tears

Book III~ Coming Soon


## Peach Coloured Daisies:
## A Cursed by the Gods Story

He couldn't die. An ancient curse meant she always did. This time, that was going to change -- one way or another.

When Daisy's grandmother, her last living relative, passes away, she doesn't know where to turn. Things go from bad to worse when a local psychic tells her about a curse. Alone and confused, she ends up in front of her college professor's office, ready to cry her heart out in his arms.

Matt Demi might be the son of a God, but he's living the life of a cursed man. He's had to watch the woman he loves die on her twenty-first birthday countless times. Nothing he does seems to be able to affect the outcome. When she shows up at his office scared out of her wits by a psychic's prediction, he vows this time will be different.

With only three days, Matt will need to embrace a side of him he swore off long ago to save her, but will he lose himself in the process?

## *Flower Shields: A Four Horsemen Novel*

Meet the four horsemen: Michael, Gabrielle, Uriel and Raphael. For centuries their job has been to guard the gates of hell, making sure they never open. Without the keys, there was never any real threat. That's about to change. There are rumours on the horizon that demon followers unearthed scrolls that explain exactly how to find the lost keys. This new battle is a race to see which side locates them first.

Michael couldn't care less about the love story behind how and why the world was created. In fact, nothing matters to him other than keeping the gates to hell closed. If one of the lost keys ever fell into the wrong hands, all humanity would be doomed. He's not going to let that happen -- at any cost.

**********

Tara's life is nothing short of a disaster. She's managed to flunk out of college with about the same amount of dignity as every relationship she's been in. The only constant in her life has been her love for flowers. When she's attacked at work, a stranger comes to her aid. Michael might be good-looking, but he's also arrogant, bossy and crazy. He's also her only chance to figure out who attacked her and why. Should she follow her heart and trust him -- or listen to her head and run?

### *Drawing Strength From Words: A Four Horsemen Novel*

Meet the four horsemen: Michael, Gabrielle, Uriel and Raphael.

For centuries their sole purpose has been guarding the sealed gates to hell. Without keys, there was never any real threat. That was about to change...

For Gabrielle, protecting mankind was merely a job for which she received little credit. The vast insecurities of men altered history itself, portraying her as a masculine brute. Taking a back seat to her brothers seemed the right thing to do, but left a bitter taste in her mouth and an impenetrable barricade shielding her heart.

**********

Ryder bounced around the system from the moment both his parents were killed. Between that and run-ins with the law for crimes he never committed, it seemed the whole world was conspiring against him. Never growing attached to anyone was rule number one: a rule he'd never broken until a white-haired vixen, with blocks of ice on her shoulders, walked right into his life. Melting through those frosty layers became all that mattered, even if that meant sacrificing himself in the process.

## Miracles Not Included

A heartfelt romantic story about: life; love; loss; and learning to love again. If only life came with instructions and a warning label ~ Miracles Not Included.

**********

Chris was born to be a writer. Even the smallest of details couldn't pass without notice, often becoming part of a plot for her next novel. The one thing she never saw coming was her husband's sudden illness.

Jason loved his wife from the moment they met. Nothing could ever change that -- nothing except the death sentence he'd been handed -- a terminal cancer diagnosis.

His story was ending: Hers was starting a new chapter and more than one miracle was needed to turn the page.

## *Twisted Tales of a Dead End Street*

A paranormal mystery laced with comedic undertones: Twisted Tales of a Dead End Street.

Nine neighbours were invited to the mysterious dinner party at 9 Nine Street. Their host, the owner of the mansion, had more planned for the evening than just roast beef.

When the secret of their quiet street was revealed, everything changed, blurring the lines between the tangible and the paranormal.

Was the number nine the difference between life and death? Would any of them survive long enough to uncover the truth? They would each soon find out this wasn't a simple case of who-done-it so much as one of what was being done and by whom.

## Shot Through The Heart: A Faerie Tale

A tale of two worlds -- one filled with magic; the other void of it. But what happened to those trapped between the two? Adelia was about to find out...

Magic and structure were the foundations of her existence. Temptation controlled the ability to destroy everything she knew. The world of men held a powerful allure over her heart, waking that which had long been dormant. It enticed her, snagging her in a web of emotions.

A decision had to be made. Was feeling love for the first time worth sacrificing magic and immortality?

## Do Not Open Until Halloween

When eighteen year old Caitlin agreed to babysit her eccentric Aunt's two cats and house, she had no idea that Justin was finally going to ask her for a date the same weekend. Torn between family and crush, she chose to take her best friends' suggestion to heart, arranging a small Friday night gathering. Little did she know a fairy was about to crash the party with trouble hot on her wings.

Caitlin will have to dig deep to find even a smidgen of belief in magic or there won't be any hope of saving her new friend from being hunted.

In this young adult fantasy, award-winning author, C.A. King, explores the answer to one of the questions readers have always wanted to ask...

Where do fairies come from?

### Truly Unfortunate

Growing up in Knoll County wasn't easy, especially without any childhood memories. Truly spent her whole life searching for the answers her mind refused to reveal. There might have been horrors in her past, but her current existence wasn't much better than a nightmare. After beginning treatments with a new doctor, disturbing visions began to resurface. The stench of death surrounded her, but where exactly was it coming from?

Jeff always knew he wanted to be one of Knoll County's finest and had no problem achieving that dream. A part of his ambition stemmed from the death of a classmate at the tender age of nine. It might have been ruled an accident, but his gut told him otherwise. When people start turning up dead in the same pattern, Jeff will be forced to put everything on the line to connect the dots between past and present. But in doing so, will his own future be jeopardized?

Truly Unfortunate is a dark paranormal thriller that will leave readers with chills after answering the question: Which is stronger... the boundaries of reality or the safety on one's own mind?

## Merry Apocalypse

For centuries, families gathered throughout the holiday season to hear recitals of the famous words of Dr. Clement C. Moore's 'Twas the Night Before Christmas and celebrate the long awaited return of Santa. His jovial generosity became synonymous with all that was Merry and bright. Then everything changed.

This year, the gatherings are sharing their own Christmas story. Merry Apocalypse includes the telling of a new traditional tale that echoes the tone and rhythm of familiar poetry, but instead of joy and bliss, contains warnings of danger and death.

### Sometimes Love Stinks

What's in a name? Everything when it's laughable.

Gastrella M. Balance was living a never-ending nightmare. For several years, she'd been the butt of jokes about... her butt. Moving to Knollville was a chance for a fresh start. It was a place where no one knew her past, or her name and she was determined to keep both a secret. Her strategy was to stay under the radar and as inconspicuous as possible. That plan, however, went south the first time she laid eyes on Tanner. When he noticed her, too, she couldn't help but hope for a bit of romance, no matter how far fetched it seemed.

*****

Tanner had everything a guy could ask for in his senior year of high school. He had a football in one hand and a pretty girl hanging off the other arm. Being popular and the center of attention came naturally to him. Taking tests, however, did not and he was desperate to keep that part of his life to himself.

When a series of pranks go awry, they'll both be faced with confronting their personal anxieties. Together, they might have a chance to overcome the odds and survive the year.

Sometimes Love Stinks is a romantic comedy that deals with issues that are both real and difficult. While the main characters in this story are from the mundane world, readers can expect to find the signature supernatural kiss C.A. King adds to all her books.

www.ingramcontent.com/pod-product-compliance
Lightning Source LLC
Chambersburg PA
CBHW031110260626
47172CB00001B/300